The Start.

This book belongs to...

_____ ____ _____ ____ ___ _____ ____ _____ ____ ____ ____

Although, apparently this is not legally binding if you just write your name in it while you're still in the book shop, before you paid for it. If it is legally binding then the security staff at Waterstone's Purley need an evening class in property law.

DEDICATIONS:

For Little Susan. Sorry about the time I sneezed in your hair. LH

For Mum, MOTHER, Tall Susan, Mrs Johnson at number 32, Natalie, Samson, Mabel and Mr Socks the cat and Janice Long. BH

To my late budgie Misty, who I miss terribly. CC ← who IS this?!

FOR MONEY MAINLY. RTP

A Doofus called "Scott" [handwritten]

The Friday Project
An imprint of HarperCollins *Publishers*
77–85 Fulham Palace Road
Hammersmith, London W6 8JB
www.harpercollins.co.uk

Love this book? www.bookarmy.com [handwritten: Yes I do!]

First published in Great Britain by The Friday Project in 2010
Copyright © Howard Read and Chris Chantler 2010

1 [handwritten: !?!?! Him Again!?!]

Howard Read and Chris Chantler assert the moral right to
be identified as the authors of this work

A catalogue record for this book
is available from the British Library [handwritten: BORING!]

978-0-00-739125-7

Designed and Typeset by Liam Relph
Photographs by Lee York

Printed and bound in Spain by
Graficas Estella

All rights reserved. No part of this publication may be
reproduced, stored in a retrieval system, or transmitted,
in any form or by any means, electronic, mechanical,
photocopying, recording or otherwise, without the prior
written permission of the publishers.

[handwritten: Don't read it in the bath either. It takes ages to dry out.]

This book is sold subject to the condition that it shall not, by way of trade or
otherwise, be lent, re-sold, hired out or otherwise circulated without the
publisher's prior consent in any form of binding or cover other than that in
which it is published and without a similar condition including this condition
being imposed on the subsequent purchaser.

[handwritten: paragraph of: blah blah blah blah blah blah. blah]

FSC

FSC is a non-profit international organisation established to promote the
responsible management of the world's forests. Products carrying the FSC
label are independently certified to assure consumers that they come from
forests that are managed to meet the social, economic and ecological needs of
present or future generations.

[handwritten: PFC is Purley football club. The two are not connected]

Find out more about HarperCollins and the environment at
www.harpercollins.co.uk/green

[handwritten: www.littlehoward.co.uk.]

GLUE PAGE 124 HERE

GLUE PAGE 124 HERE

CONTENTS

Front – brilliant picture of me, possibly with Big Howard on as well.
Inside cover-bit – Monkey song lyrics.
Flappy pointless pages before proper book – a load of addresses and numbers and stuff.
1....... This page, obviously
2 – Big Howard's Introduction (I'd skip this if I were you)
4 – My Brilliant introduction
6....... erm...
7....... Maybe something about mice?
8....... A really great drawing I did when I was on holiday
9....... Don't know
10...
11...
12...

DON'T KNOW! How are we supposed to know what's on every page of the book?! We haven't written it yet, have we!? My publisher's an idiot!

The only bit we're definite about is this:

124...... CONTENTS – we're going to do the contents at the end, because we can't do it now because we don't know what's going to be in the book – duh.

In fact; What you should do if you REALLY want the contents at the front is cut out page 124 and stick it in here with Sticky Stick Glue Stick (The Glue So Safe It Doesn't Work). I've even done the dotted lines and everything for you. Do we really have to do everything for you?!

Lots of love, Little Howard

'AN INTRODUCTION'
BY BIG HOWARD

Dear Esteemed Reader,

Big Howard here, wishing you a warm welcome to LITTLE HOWARD'S BIG BOOK. In it I would like to tell you all the stuff I know and have learned in my long and interesting life. I say long, I'm actually still very young. In spite of what the media, Wikipedia and my mum might say, I am not Thirty-five, I am twenty-three. I just didn't start moisturizing until very late in life.

This book is going to be great. It's going to allow you little people to glimpse into the magical world of this business we call Show Business!

But it's not all fascinatingly interesting and heart-poundingly exciting in this life, you know. For example, at the moment I'm sitting in my car (a silver Ford Focus Zetec – none of your rubbish, I got it second-hand, one careful owner and quite low mileage) in the car park of Heston Service Station typing this on my laptop. Heston services is the one between junction 2 and 3 of the M4, I'm on the way back from visiting my Aunt Linda. It's got a Costa Coffee and a WH Smiths! Heston Services that is, not my Aunt Linda. I wanted a coffee and a pen, so with its Costa/WH Smiths combination I thought 'It's Heston Services for me!'

But I didn't just want a coffee and a pen, I also wanted to write something down. As a writer you should always have a pen because you might have a brilliant idea any minute! I hadn't had any brilliant or fascinating ideas since last May fantastic idea wasn't a joke or anything, it was an invention! at he It was underwear that kept you warm! owl he began to experiment with lots of closer investigation someone nvented by a man called Count Rumford ermal underwear but it wasn't just a Rumfor vented Rumford soup and introduced

Big Howard?

something altogeth... ...Their... ...wear was commissioned
for all sorts of ...1914!... ...he need thermal
underwear for!? ... a much ...ficient way to heat
a ro... th... ...eated a ser... in London... hen he
...g the chimney op...in... to increase
...is workers changed fireplaces... ...erting bricks
...the side walls angled... ...added a choke to the chim...
...ed of air... ...ively produced
...ow, ...he chimney rath...
...enter ...esidents. It al
...of i... ...nd gave extra
...London houses...
...e. Thompson became a celebr...
...s also very profitable, an...
...he way chimneys worked. In...
...he also invented a new k...
...flow into and throug...ace... a

commun...ed to the barrel
...attempt to f... ...enerated o...
...of heat. Though this work...
...important ...est...
...centu...
It w... ...urprise a...st...
...eei... large a qu...
...with... any fire.

Perhaps Count Rumford not only invented thermal underwear, introduced the potato to Bavaria and refined the design of the coffee pot, but also invented a machine that could look into the future and read my mind?!! How else did a man who lived two hundred years ago copy my idea of inventing thermal underwear!?

Big Howard?

What?!

This introduction of yours...

What about it?!

Well...it's a bit boring, isn't it?

What do you mean! I bet YOU didn't know who introduced the potato to Bavaria!? Look you've covered up the whole rest of the page!

I'm sure we're not missing anything.

Shut up for a minute and we'll find out.

I'd like to see YOU do a better introduction!

See? Drivel! You're supposed to be introducing the book, not droning on about a man who introduced himself to potatoes and invented warm pants.

Fine!

So would I. I'll do one on the next page.

Oh dear. I've run out of space.

LITTLE HOWARD'S INTRODUCTION

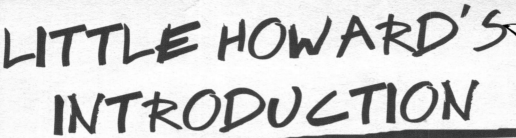

Whelk Omm!

Hello! Welcome to LITTLE HOWARD'S BIG BOOK. Big Howard wanted to write an 'inspirational book of knowledge and wisdom' called BIG HOWARD'S LITTLE BOOK but that's a stupid idea, I think you'll agree. I'm not even 100% sure that's what he said, I couldn't hear because I was shouting 'BORING! BORING! BORING!' as loud as I could while he was describing it to me. He has gone to the shed to sulk, which I think is quite childish.

LITTLE HOWARD'S BIG! BOOK!!

entirely written by LITTLE HOWARD!!!

(this is a sausage)

BLAH BLAH

BORING! BORING! BORING!

This book is going to be BRILLIANT. It is probably going to be the best book you've ever read. I'm particularly excited because I don't know what's going to be in it either!

Our publisher said we haven't given ourselves enough time to write this book properly and we should have spent the last four months writing this book, instead of playing table tennis. But what does he know?! I don't even know what a 'publisher' is! It sounds like someone who spends a lot of time in pubs. Maybe licking them? And he's been licking pubs so long that his tongue is all sore from the rough bricks and he can't even say 'Pub-Licker' properly anymore!

Our publisher keeps on saying that books need 'planning' and 're-drafting' and we have to look at all the pages we've written again and again and again and again. But I think we should just write it, starting at page 1 and finishing at page _ however many pages there are supposed to be. That's how you read a book, so why should writing a book be any different?! There's no need to look at what we've written because we know it's going to be brilliant! (Well, my bits will be, and I can always just draw really good pictures over Big Howard's pages.)

The worst thing in the world is if you're reading a book and someone gives away what happens at the end. Well with my way of doing things that can NEVER HAPPEN, because even I don't know what's going to happen in the end! We might not even finish it! That'd be a twist-in-the-tail!

I hope you enjoy reading our book, just as much as I hope I enjoy writing it.

LITTLE HOWARD

So, erm, we've welcomed you twice. Welcome. Three times now. And we've done the contents so just 124 pages to fill... erm... Little Howard, you have a go.

Hello, Little Howard here. Erm... I... Two monkeys walk into a... no...

Look, this is the truth of it: it might look like we haven't done any work and we've only got three days to start and finish the book, but we have had LOADS of ideas, but our stupid pub-licker says that none of them will work. Here is PROOF that I at least have done loads of preparation for this book. The brilliant handwriting is mine, the rubbish handwriting is our pub-licker's.

LITTLE HOWARD's book ideas!

1. Can the book do a little guff when you open it?
   – NO – THE PUBLISHER

2. How big can we make the book? As big as a garage door?!
   – IT IS A4. ANY BIGGER YOU HAVE TO PAY.

3. Can we do some pages in sandpaper? –NO

4. Edible rice paper? – NO

5. Greaseproof paper? – NO

6. Could some pages be made of metal? –NO

7. Stretched goatskin? – NO

8. Could the front page be made of wood? –NO

9. Could we write the book in invisible ink? or say we have, and publish it now?
   – NO. ALTHOUGH THIS MIGHT MAKE FOR A BETTER BOOK.

As you can see, I am being creatively stifled, so if this book is rubbish it is NOT MY FAULT, it is his.

Oo! Big Howard says he's got an idea for what we're going to do on the next page! Phew!

Long Neck Jeff had a terribly long neck.

Long Neck Jeff

by Big Howard.

Long Neck Jeff's amazingly long neck meant he could see right up very high, and around corners and stuff!

But overstretching his neck caused it quite serious damage, and Long Neck Jeff had to wear a neck brace (or forty-one neck braces, because of his very long neck!) for upwards of six weeks.

Big Howard?

But then, Extraordinarily Wide-Headed Barry reached out his hand from under his extraordinarily wide head and felt a spot of rain!

Would you like to borrow my umberella, Long Neck Jeff?

Gargle, gargle, gargle, gargle.

Oh! Long Neck Jeff!

That was a true story and if you want to give any money to people like Long Neck Jeff who suffer from the rare disease of er... Giraffism then send your money to Roger T. Pigeon, who's in charge of (let me work it out...) S.O.P.A.G: The Society Of Pigeons Against Giraffism.

As much money as you can spare please, in used notes. Just bung it under my door in a bag, and make sure the fuzz aren't watching.

S.O.P.A.G
The Society Of Pigeons Against Giraffism

Big Howard's
Guide to Writing

Whether you're writing a story, a novel, a comic book or a bit of homework, you can't just sit down and write it! You have to prepare. Whether you're staring at a blank page, an essay title, the opening scene of an opera, or even a great big book you and your cartoon friend have got to fill by the end of the month or you won't get paid – YOU NEED TO READ THIS! Instead of writing that.

1. NO DISTRACTIONS

The worst enemy of a writer is procrastination. If you don't know what that means, go and look it up before you start work… Actually, I don't know what it means…

Hang on…

…Sorry about the wait. I've looked it up, Procrastination means: *verb*, [intrans]. delay or postpone action; put off doing something. Now we've all done that, haven't we?! As I was saying, putting things off, or procrastination is the writer's worst enemy. So here are some tips to make sure NOTHING can distract you from your work!!!

2. FOCUS!!!!!!!

If you've got any chores your parents have been nagging you to do, do them before you start trying to write, for heaven's sake! There's nothing worse than getting halfway through a really good first word when someone tells you that you haven't cleaned the car. If your parents, wife or animated boy haven't given you anything to do, then do some stuff they might ask you to do at some point. That way they won't be able to distract you! Go around the house making sure all the pictures are straight. You might notice that the living room needs hoovering. Do it now, or you'll never get started on your writing!

3. NEVER WRITE HUNGRY!

So before you sit down to write make yourself a nice meal. Perhaps your favourite snack, or a Pot Noodle if you're not that great at cooking, or have no tastebuds. You might need to go to the shops; the last thing you want when writing a book is an empty fridge. Make sure you've got everything you need - hummus, eggs, exotic fruit, gonks, Power Rangers, etc.

3. HYDRATION, HYDRATION, HYDRATION!

The next part is crucial: DESCALE THE KETTLE!! The last thing you want hanging over your head when trying to write a book is limescale in your kettle. After this, you may as well test the kettle by making a nice cup of tea. This will help prevent you becoming dehydrated during your long writing stint. If you don't drink tea, perhaps go and buy something you do drink, or try drinking tea, it's lovely.

4. GET THE RIGHT EQUIPMENT!

They say 'a bad workman blames his tools,' but I've found, more often than not, it is the tool's fault. If you're not happy with your pen, or your pencil, or your computer, for heaven's sake don't start writing until you've got one you're happy with. If this means putting off your homework until you've saved up enough money for a top-of-the-range laptop, then so be it. No teacher in their right mind will give you a detention for that!

And here's a tip. If you usually write using a computer, it can sometimes be inspiring to do it the old-fashioned way and use a pen. It's quite hard to hit the right keys on the keyboard typing with a pen, but it's worth it! If it's good enough for Dickens, it's good enough for me. If that doesn't work for you, why not go back even further and use a quill. This might involve catching some sort of bird, a swan or a goose perhaps, then making one of their feathers into a pen and typing with that.

5. OKAY, SO NOW YOU'RE READY TO WRITE!

Now, and only now, can you sit down to write your book, essay or letter to the *Daily Mail*. But for goodness sake, MAKE SURE you've checked your e-mail first. The last thing you want hanging over your head when writing is an inbox full of unchecked e-mails.

6. RELAX! ... RELAX! ... RELAAAX!

At this point, some people like to go for a nice walk. Walking often helps to clear your mind of all those writing worries. If you get distracted, and end up at the cinema, or in the pub, don't let that stress you out. A writer's life is about being spontaneous and free!

When you get back make sure you CLEAN YOUR SHOES!

7. I'M HUNGRY

It might be lunch time now. Again, you must NEVER WRITE HUNGRY. So perhaps go out for a nice lunch in a local pub or café. If you've just been to the pub during the previous stage, maybe choose a different pub. You can get so much inspiration just listening to people and the way they speak. And playing on the arcade games.

8. WHEN TO WRITE?

The afternoon is the best time to write, I imagine. You've got all those jobs out of the way, and you're completely free to sit down, with the telly on, and WRITE THAT BOOK! Often inspiration doesn't come immediately, so perhaps watch telly for a bit if you're struggling. How can you call yourself a writer if you don't immerse yourself in REAL life? And *Deal Or No Deal*?

9. GET YOUR SLEEP!

When I've woken up after falling asleep watching *Deal Or No Deal* I'm often too groggy to write, and I go to bed for forty winks. After my 'POWER NAP', as I call it, I'm all ready to write. Sleeping is HUGELY important to the writer. It doesn't just keep you relaxed and clear thinking, you might have a dream while you're asleep! You never know you might dream a whole book. That's what Mary Shelley did, who wrote *Frankenstein* (I think) and then of course there's Daphne Du Maurier's bestselling classic *Why am I Naked in Sainsburys?* NEVER BE ASHAMED OF SLEEP!

10. WATCH *HOME AND AWAY*

All writers watch *Home and Away*. It really is essential. You can't be a writer unless you're right up to date with the plot of *Home and Away*. It's kind of a writer's exercise. If *Home and Away* isn't on at the moment, maybe go on the internet and look up YouTube clips of old episodes. Or perhaps order a boxset, and watch all of that.

14. KNOW WHEN TO STOP!

By now it's probably tea time. I never write after dark, because it's bad for your eyes. So I watch telly instead. Then I go to bed, because nothing is more important to a writer than SLEEP!

A Note from the Publisher

Dear Reader,

There seems to have been a bit of a mistake. It wasn't my fault. I was on a skiing holiday in Holland. I must admit I did miss some calls from the office while I was there, but I was too busy (trying to find the ski lift, and then making angry phone calls to my travel agent after someone told me, laughing rather unkindly, that Holland was almost entirely flat, and therefore not very good for downhill skiing) to answer them.

Basically, what has happened is that this book has been printed before it was finished. It's a mess, it really is. I hate it. It's awful. There's scribble all over some of the pages, someone's drawn moustaches on some of the pictures, and several very interesting essays have been completely ruined, or covered up with a napkin that someone had done a childish drawing all over.

What happened was there was some disagreement amongst the authors of this book as to what sort of book it should be. Howard Read, known to some as Big Howard thought it should be called *Big Howard's Little Book*, a very educational tome, that would edify and inform its young readers with insight and knowledge from his 'very very educated brain'. The other author, Little Howard, thought Big Howard didn't have a 'very very educated brain' and that the book should be full of lots of daft stuff that would make people laugh. He thought it should be called *Little Howard's Big Book*.

They never really agreed which it should be, and set about writing their own book and trying to sabotage each other's work to make it more/less educational and less/more funny.

Our editors were trying to make it into a book that made sense when someone, we don't know who, bundled it up and sent it the printers before it was finished with a note attached saying 'Print This Now You Great Flan'.

All I can do is apologize for this terrible mistake. And what makes me most sorry of all is that you've bought it without reading this. Oh well, I've got your money now, that is a shame, and you won't be able to get your money back because… erm… I've rubbed some mud on the bottom corner of this page – look. It's ruined. No book shop would ever take it back.

I do hope you can enjoy this book even though it's a terrible mess and it makes no sense whatsoever.

Scott Pack

Scott Pack
Publisher
The Friday Project

The Friday Project . HarperCollins Publishers . 77-85 Fulham Palace Road . London . W6 8JB

www.thefridayproject.co.uk

Big Howard
& Little Howard's
WORLD
ATLAS

Part 1 - some bits of Britain that we've been to.

We had no idea what to do on the next page, and then *Big Howard* sneezed, and the bogey landed on the table cloth and it was EXACTLY the same shape as the Isle of Skye!

So I had a brilliant idea what we could do next!

Unfortunately it turns out that *Big Howard* hasn't got a natural gift for doing greenies in the shape of geographical features. And it turns out he can't sneeze on command. I had to throw pepper in his face, several times.

His second sneeze looked a bit like a dog. But one that didn't have enough legs.

And his last sneeze, before he took the pepper away from me, looked like Miley Cyrus, which is USELESS when you're trying to get someone to sneeze a map of the British Isles.

So instead *Big Howard* and me have <u>drawn</u> a map of the British Isles, which isn't anywhere near as much fun. Apparently we got some of it wrong, and Scott our ~~Pub-licker~~ has spoilt it a bit by changing some of what we've written. The Big Flanhead.

I'm a Publisher!!

MAP OF BRITAIN

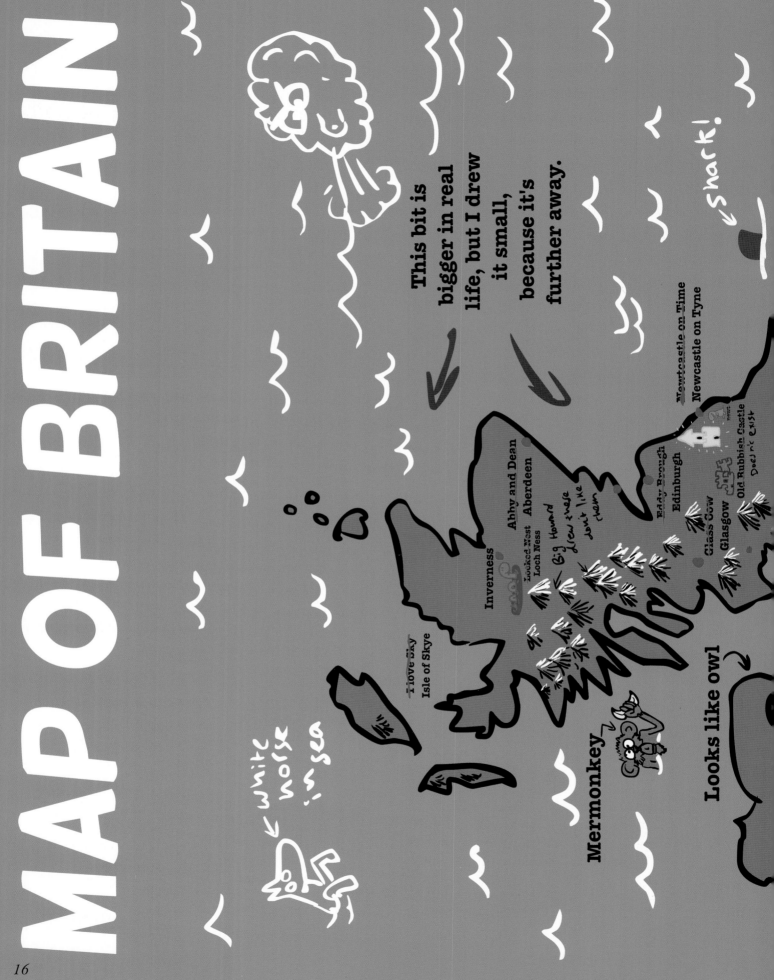

This bit is bigger in real life, but I drew it small, because it's further away.

White noise in sea

I love you
Isle of Skye

Inverness

Looked West
Loch Ness

Abby and Dean
Aberdeen

Big Howard
drew these
don't like them

Mermonkey

Looks like owl

Eady Brough
Edinburgh

Glass Cow
Glasgow

Old Rubbish Castle
Does it exist

Newcastle on Time
Newcastle on Tyne

shark!

A-Z OF BRITAIN

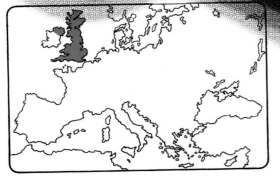

0 20 40 60 80 100 Kilometres

0   25   50
Miles   █ = Britain

B (Bee)

BATH, Somerset
Bath's original name was 'The Only Town In England With A Bath', but it was shortened, obviously. Yes, in the old days, there was only one bath in the whole country, and it was here. It became very popular. The Queen came every Sunday after *Antiques Roadshow*. They had to do a rota – as a result of which, nobody up north was allowed to have a bath until the 1950s. Until then they had to make do with a Black Pool.

BIDEFORD, Devon
A ford is a shallow part of a river where it is safe to cross. And a Bidet is something the French use for washing their bottoms. So at Bideford they used to wash their bottoms in the ford. It became known as the Bidet Ford, and the 't' was shot off the sign during a war.

BRADFORD, Yorkshire
Bradford is named Bradford because the people believed that one day Brad Pitt would marry Harrison Ford. It hasn't happened yet, but they're pretty sure it will.

BUXTON, Derbyshire
Buxton was originally called Box Town, because all the houses were made out of cardboard. But now it's called Buxton, because they've all got LOADS of money.

C (See)

CARDIFF, South Glamorganshire
Cardiff was named because the person naming it was trying to call the town 'Cardi', but sadly a book fell on his head at the wrong moment. Cardiff has a restraining order out against Doctor Who, for a while there he just WOULDN'T leave the place alone.

CHESTER, Cheshire
The sister town to Manchester. Strictly no-boys-allowed, every male in Chester has to move to Manchester.

D (Dee)

DUMFRIES, Dumfries & Galloway
Dumfries, translated directly means 'stupid chips'. No one knows why, because the chips in Dumfries are actually really clever.

E (Eeeeeeeeee)

EDINBURGH
Was named after it found someone called Ed in an iceberg.

F (Eff)

FALMOUTH, Cornwall
Falmouth is called Falmouth because the people in Falmouth are very very rude.

G (Jee)

GLASGOW, Scotland
Glasgow is of course named after a glass cow that used to live here, until it was smashed by CLUMSY ENGLISH PEOPLE!

H (Bch)

HARROGATE, Yorkshire
Harrogate is named after a very scary gate... it's the gate out of Yorkshire. Or in to Yorkshire, depending on where you're from.

HASTINGS, West Sussex
Haystings is called that because everyone there is allergic to hay. It was called 'Hay Is Quite Itchy' but they shortened it because the last word kept falling off the sign.

I (Eye)

INVERNESS, Inverness-shire
Inverness is called Inverness, because the whole town used to be 'In A Nest'. It changed to Inverness because people there used to mumble quite a lot.

L (Ell)

LAND'S END, Cornwall
Originally, when the people who first discovered Britain arrived at the very tip of Cornwall they called it Land's Beginning, because that's where the country started. Then they went all round Britain and back out the way they came and at that point they changed its name to Land's End, because they were leaving it, and sent news back to the gift shop saying they had to reprint all their sticks of rock.

LONDON, Greater London
London was originally named Lonnie Donnegan, but it got shortened like Jennifer Lopez shortened her name to J-Lo, and Barney Harwood shortened his to Ba-Ha.

M (Emm)

MANCHESTER, Greater Manchester
Manchester was originally (in the Olden Days) the overspill town of Chester, who instituted a no-boys-allowed policy and sent all the fellas off on a boat.

P (Pee!)

PETERBOROUGH, Cambridgeshire
Peterborough used to be called 'Bury Peter', and everybody called Peter had to be buried on a certain day of the year, or it was thought to bring bad luck. True story.

R (Arrrrgh)

READING, Berkshire
Reading was the first of the Three R's towns planned in the 1800s. They ran out of money though before they could build Riting and Rithmatic.

RHYL, Denbighshire
Rhyl used to be called 'Drill' but the D got washed out to sea. The sea then added an 'H' and a 'Y', somehow.

P (Pee!)

PURLEY, Surrey
Purley was named after what Cilla Black said when she was feeling sorry for someone called Lee, who was from the Purley area, when he was appearing on her TV show *Surprise Surprise*. She said 'Uuuur Puur Lee!' (which means 'Ahh, Poor Lee' in Cilla) then she said 'I'm soooo Surrey, give 'im a round of applause!'. Before that Purley wasn't even in Surrey.

T (Tea)

TAUNTON, Somerset
The people of Taunton are traditionally not very nice to tourists. Whenever visitors arrived they would immediately be taunted by townsfolk. 'Go on, get out of it you not-from-round-here nitwit,' they'd shout, and 'Your wife looks like a weasel' and things like that. People from nearby used to say, 'Ha-harr, don't go round there unless you want a tauntin', me lad, ha-harr.' Because they were all pirates.

TRING, Hertfordshire
Where bicycle bells are made.

TUNBRIDGE WELLS, Kent
Tunbridge Wells was named after all the bridges that all weigh exactly a tonne, and some wells. The European Union wanted it to change its name to Onepointzeroonesixkilogrammebridge Wells. But everyone made a fuss.

W (Double-you)

WESTON-SUPER-MARE, Somerset
Weston – called Weston because it's a town in the west (zzz) – was a very boring sleepy little place... until Supermare arrived! Supermare was a kind of horse with magic powers. He totally transformed the place. Suddenly there were fish and chip shops and ice cream vans and variety shows on the end of the pier. They added 'Supermare' to the town's name in his honour, and every summer tourists flooded in from all over the country. It's dried up a bit now, to be honest.

WINCHESTER, Hampshire
Winchester is named, of course, after the time they had to get a girl called Esther out because she fell down a well.

Z (Zed)

Before we finally got on telly we were writing to loads of channels with loads of ideas for new programmes, but every single one was rejected. Here are some of the ideas that you didn't get a chance to see because TV bosses are so rubbish!

ALL-STAR CELEBRITY HOPSCOTCH

A team of all-star celebrity girls jump over a chalk grid while singing weird songs. A team of all-star celebrity boys watches them from a distance wondering what the gibbing flump they're doing.

MAINLY LITTLE SUSAN'S IDEA

THE NEWS WITH CUSTARD PIES

A newsreader says what's happening in the world while being pelted with gooey eggy tarts.

A BIG HOWARD/LITTLE HOWARD CO-PRODUCTION

LITTLE SUSAN'S STEAM TRAIN SUMO ADVENTURE

Twenty-four part documentary tracing Little Susan's journey round the world on a steam train to watch lots of sumo wrestling.

NOTHING TO DO WITH ME

PIGEON IN NEED/PIGEON RELIEF/PIGEON AID

Roger begs people to send him enough money to buy a hot tub, a speedboat, and a working fleet of Daleks.

THIS WAS ROGER'S IDEA

DINOSAURS VS SPACE ALIENS

At last, we find out who's hardest! Filmed entirely on location in space, we were hoping to get David Attenborough to do the voiceover.

ALL-STAR CELEBRITY WHO CAN HOLD THEIR BREATH THE LONGEST?

Fifteen celebrities compete for the coveted title of Celebrity Who Can Hold Their Breath The Longest. This might need some work, now I look at it.

ALL-STAR CELEBRITY I-SPY

Three celebrities are crammed into the back of a Peugeot and driven around the motorway system of Great Britain while playing I-Spy.

THE COMPUTER-BASED CHAT SHOW

Basically, computers interviewing famous people. In the first episode a Dell PC asks Lady Gaga if she's writing a letter, if she wants to save her password, and if she's sure she wants to force quit.

GUESS WHOSE IDEA THIS WAS

I hope nobody notices that you're so desperate to fill pages you fished these ideas out of the bin.

THE NEWS WITH FISH DOWN TROUSERS

A newsreader says what's happening in the world while having trout forced down his pants.

THE NEWS DANGLING FROM A LEDGE

A newsreader says what's happening in the world while dangling precariously from a ledge. Will he fall off before the weather forecast?

We nearly got away with it!

Little Howard's
DUNG OF
THE NEW FOREST

A Pictorial Study in Crayons and Coloured Pencils by Little Howard

LH Press

～🐉 INTRODUCTION 🐉～

Hello, and welcome to the first collection of my brilliant art pictures. I am often asked, 'WHY have you just drawn lots of pictures of poo, Little Howard, for goodness' sakes? WHY?' And I say, 'Aah, the person looking at the pictures has to work it out for themselves, aah.' And then they say, 'What? That's not an answer,' and I say, 'Aaah' a few more times and try and look clever, and they go off scratching their heads.

In fact, Big Howard and I went to the New Forest recently for a mini-break and I bought some new coloured pencils and we went for lots of walks and I noticed two things: a) the New Forest is very pretty and b) it is full of a wide variety of poos. I also noticed that if I brought my coloured pencils and a sketch pad and sat down and drew pictures, Big Howard would agree to stop talking.

So here it is, *Dung of The New Forest*, the result of literally minutes of hard but quite fun work. If this goes well I'm thinking of releasing a second book, *Plops of The Pennines*.

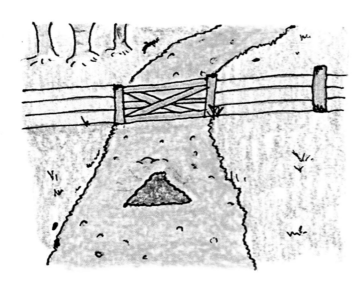

(*Left*) **Steaming mound of pony doings, approaching Holly Hatch Enclosure**
The New Forest pony is the guv'nor of the New Forest – literally. A pony parliament meets once a year to discuss pony-based issues – mostly just to confirm that they can still go poo-poos anywhere they like. So do tread carefully.

(*Left*) **Cowpats in bloom at Matley Holms**
In the old days in the New Forest, when it was slightly newer, the villagefolk used to use cowpats as frisbees. Big Howard thinks that's a good idea, 'cos they wouldn't hurt so much when they hit him on the head at high speed.

(*Above*) **Roe plops at Roe Enclosure**
Roe is a species of small reddish-brown deer, and also a word for fish eggs. Roe Enclosure got its name obviously because fish lay their eggs in the trees. And there are lots of deer here too, as you can see by this pic of their plops.

(*Right*) ***Illegal*** **doggy mess at Rakes Brakes Bottom**
Lovely spot, Rakes Brakes Bottom: the stream, the heather, the gentle hills, the HORRID STINKING DOG MESS THAT YOU'RE SUPPOSED TO TAKE HOME AND DISPOSE OF PROPERLY. Tsk.

can cause blindness.

(*Above*) **Pigeon splats on sketch pad at Woodfidley**
(Damn you, Roger!)

(*Left*) **Otter pats by Dockens Water**
Otters are surprisingly messy, and their poos are surprisingly dark. Maybe they eat a lot of liquorice. It's rare to see otters in the forest, but not so rare to see their hard, curly black number twos beside a lovely stream.

(*Below*) **Colossal heap of elephant dung next to Ocknell Pond**
Oh, all right, I made Big Howard drive it there from the zoo. Lovely spot for it, though!

Little Howard's Song Lyrics

I HAVE TO GO TO SLEEP

BIG HOWARD
Sleep will calm you…
Bed will rest you…

LITTLE HOWARD
I have got to go to sleep.
Go to bed or go insane,
After several days awake,
I have found it hard to take,
Control back of my brain.

I have got to close my eyes,
Close the door upon the day.
After several days alert,
My head has started to hurt,
Drop off and float away.

SLEEP EXPERT
And I can answer your question,
Of why you go to bed,
That's if you don't you'll go out of your head!

BIG HOWARD AND SLEEP EXPERT
Sleep will calm you…
Bed will rest you…

LITTLE HOWARD
I have got to have a kip.
Let my brain rest for the night.
I need more than forty winks,
That is what the expert thinks,
For my head to wake up right.

I have got to go to bed,
Go to sleep or go berserk,
It is not coincidental,
That I've been a little mental,
And my legs no longer work.

SLEEP EXPERT
For sleep's your mind's little playground,
And dreams its cinema,
Bed bugs are the extras,
You're the star!

LITTLE HOWARD
I have got to go to sleep.
Go to bed or go insane,
After several days awake,
I have found it hard to take,
Control back…
[falls asleep]

BIG HOWARD
Sleep will calm you…
Bed will rest you…

WHAT THE GIBBING FLUMP ARE YOU ON ABOUT DORIS?

LITTLE HOWARD
What the gibbing flump are you on about Doris?
What is that they say about a 'gift how-es'?
Oh I never ever understand a word you say,
I guess it doesn't really matter anyway,
Oh Doris...
Yeeeah Doris.

Oh what the blummin' flip are you on about Doris?
They say you can't see the trees for all of the forest?
You never really made a lot of sense to me,
I guess I'm gonna have to just say let it be,
Oh Doris!
Yeah Doris.

How do you like them apples?
They don't fall far from the tree.
An apple a day keeps the doctor away,
But it's never really made very much sense to me,
Oh Doris.
Mmm Doris.

What the flippin' 'eck are you gabbing' on Doris?
You musta really confused your late husband Maurice.
They say the early bird catches the early worm,
Your Maurice must have been really concerned –
About Doris.
Oh Doris.

FLYING SONG

INTRO

BIG HOWARD: Up there,
Look at him float off without a care,
Drifting like a bin bag in the air,
He pretty much go anywhere,
Up there.

LITTLE HOWARD: Fly.
All I wanted to do was to fly,
Now it seems that I'm about to die,
Falling like a stone down from the sky,
Oh why.

CHORUS

Because falling it is natural,
Flying it is not.
Oh gravity has news for me,
That cannot be forgot.

VERSE

Aeroplane, or helicopter, when I land I'll need a doctor,
Jetpack me direct to A & E.
Growing wings could be a curse,
unless they flew me to a nurse,
an NHS one please, 'cos they are free.

Hovercraft or lead balloon, please get me to a doctor soon,
float me with a magnet to a quack
and then when I've convalesced,
I'll tell you what would be the best,
please don't even try to fly me back.

CHORUS

Flying it is easy,
it's landing that I fear,
I hope that when I reach the ground,
there's a paramedic near.

VERSE

If I take off by nuclear fission,
fly me to a pediatrician,
blow me with a fan to my GP.
If I master levitation, I'll probably need an operation
float me on a cloud to A & E.

CHORUS

Because flying it is easy,
it's landing that's the worst,
I hope I'm near a hospital,
when the bubbles burst.

SPOKEN: Aaargh! They're popping the balloons! They're trying to kill me!
Ooo! No, I'm going down! They've saved me! The seagulls have saved me!

CHORUS

Because falling it is natural,
flying it is not.
Oh gravity has news for me,
that cannot be forgot.

IS THERE ANYBODY OUT THERE?

LITTLE HOWARD

Is there anybody out there,
If there is, could you please
Come and take Big Howard,
'Cos he's never really been to space,
He is big but he's easily overpowered.

BIG HOWARD

If there's anybody out there,
I'd be grateful if you stayed out there at home,
I don't want to go on holiday,
I'd be happy with a fortnight out in Rome.

LITTLE HOWARD

If there's anybody out there,
Could you please come here
And take my friend,
Show him all of the universe,
Buy him dinner at the restaurant at the end.

BIG HOWARD

If there's anybody out there,
I'd like to tell you that I'm happy where I am,
And you wouldn't really like me much,
I'm a rotter, I'd be better off in Rotterdam.

BOTH

Ahhh ahhhh.
Ahhh ahhhh.

LITTLE HOWARD

If there's anybody out there,
Take him to your leader just for me,
'Cos he's never really been to space,
And he doesn't let me watch enough TV.

BIG HOWARD

If there's anybody out there,
I'd be grateful if you stayed right where you are,
Cos I get a little travel sick,
I'd be very sick if I travelled that far.

LITTLE HOWARD

If there's anybody out there,
Show him all of the stars and a black hole,
'Cos he's never really been to space,
And he always hogs the remote control.

BIG HOWARD

(spoken)
What? Is that what all this is about? I wouldn't let you watch
that film last night. I recorded it, I forgot to tell you.
You can watch it when we get home.

LITTLE HOWARD

Oh… erm…

BOTH

If there's anybody out there,
We are very sorry to have bothered you,
Carry on invading stars,
Going shopping, or whatever it is you do.

If there's anybody out there,
Please ignore all the things that we just said,
Carry on assimilating Mars,
Tumble-drying, or perhaps just stay in bed.
Staaaay… In… Bed!

£18.23 UK

The London Review OF CRISPS

PURLEY EDITION ISSUE 01

Welcome!

Hello, I'm not allowed to eat that many packets of crisps a day, because Big Howard says they're bad for me, and if I eat too many our TV show will only be watchable in widescreen. So I've only reviewed a few bags of crisps.

But have *you* had a GREAT packet of crisps lately? Or a terrible bowl of nibbles? Or maybe you've even tasted a cornchip at a party once and you've never been able to track down who made it? Do you want to tell us, and The World about them? (NB: I'm not sure how many people will read this, so I don't think we can claim that The World will hear your opinions – we can only claim that The Entire Known World will hear your opinions.) Well, you can't, because this is a book. But if you want to you could go to www.londonreviewofcrisps.com and post your review!

Finally: Why *The London Review of Crisps?* We don't live in London, we live in Purley, just south of London, but we thought we'd call it *The London Review of Crisps* to make it sound official and important. Otherwise I don't think people would take us seriously.

Crisp Tasting Techniques

THIS IS THE TRADITIONAL WAY OF TASTING CRISPS TO BEST GET THE FULL SMELL, TASTE, 'MOUTH-FEEL' AND TEXTURE OF THE CRISP

BAD CRISPS!

You're probably like me and you probably work hard for your money. Pestering Big Howard to give it to me is a *tough* job. After a hard day's poking Big Howard and going 'Please, Big Howard, pleeeease,' Howard and putting smashed up biscuits in his pants drawer if he doesn't, I'm sure you don't want to see your pocket money wasted on BAD CRISPS!

After a particularly bad packet of Salt and Vinegar from a Tesco's multi-pack (it had six crisps in it?! How are you supposed to survive on that if you don't eat the rubbish Big Howard's cooked for your supper?!?) I decided to get in touch with my Member of Parliament and complain. Here's what he wrote back!

Dear Mr L. Howard,

Thank you for your enquiry regarding the packet of crisps you bought from Tesco. I'm sorry to hear that it only had six crisps in it. I hope it won't change the way you vote in the forthcoming election.

I'd like to point out that crisps numbers have increased by almost 15% under this administration, whereas figures showed that crisp numbers decreased markedly when the opposition was in power. We, as a government, have fought very hard to tackle the low-crisp count problem in supermarket multi-packs and are very sorry to see that low crisp-count bags are still getting through to you, the voter. Can I ask whether they were big crisps? Or was it six little ones? Because six massive crisps, all intact, is surely better than loads of tiny smashed up crisp crumbs. Please vote for me. Please.

I hope this is of some help to you at this troubling time. If you have any further concerns regarding crisps you might try contacting the

The Hula Hoop: The Great Divider

I'm not sure I'd want to live in a world where I couldn't fit Hula Hoops on my fingers and eat them like crunchy rings. But many people in the world have to live through this hell EVERY DAY! Big Howard, for example, has massive flappy hands, like a gangly frog, and he hasn't been able to fit Hula Hoops on his fingers for years now. He has to make do with whittling out the inside of the larger brand of Monster Munch, and eating them off his fingers instead!

To add in-salt-and-vinegar to injury Big Howard's nose is also too big to stick Chip Sticks up, without them falling out and/or him trying to hit me with a flying slipper. Obviously Hula Hoops are best served off your fingers, but here are some other suggestions if you've got great-big wangery

1) Put a peanut in the hole in the Hula Hoop, and eat it like a crunchy stuffed olive (WARNING! This recipe contains peanuts, one, so don't attempt to make it if you're allergic to peanuts!) (It also contains Hula Hoops, one, so don't attempt to make it if you're allergic to Hula Hoops) (It probably contains quite a lot of air between the Hula-Hoop and the peanut – if you're allergic to air, don't eat them either). Phew, glad we got that cleared up.

2) Filled with cream cheese, hummus, peanut butter (WARNING! peanut butter may contain peanuts – unless you buy the really cheap stuff), butter, margarine. Stuff the hole with Chip Sticks, French Fries or any other long thin sort of crisp, or maybe attempt to force in a Wotsit.

3) Try to flatten the Hula Hoop out so that it's normal crisp shape. I've tried doing this with an iron, getting Big Howard to reverse the car over it, and putting it under a fat man on the bus, and none of them work. The fat man ate the Hula Hoops too.

4) Try to dissolve them in Orange Juice. (NB: This is revolting and doesn't work at all, neither does the flattening thing, I just thought only putting three suggestions was a bit rubbish.

5) Eat Hula Hoops off of Chocolate Fingers instead – savoury course followed by sweet. Please note: In the interests of balance we should say there are other short-tube-shaped crisps available on the market (but they are not as good as Hula Hoops).

FEATURED CRISP OF THE WEEK:
The Prawn Cocktail Crisp.

A Prawn Cocktail crisp, taking a dip in... some dip.

Some Prawn Cocktail crisps lounging seductively on a tablecloth.

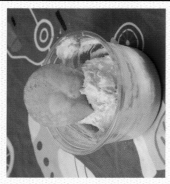

A Prawn Cocktail crisp enjoying the company of one of its primitive ancestors, the prawn. The prawn is in danger of extinction because of its inability to fit in a silver-foil multi-pack for months on end, or make a crunching noise if you bang it on the table.

SERVING SUGGESTIONS OF THE DAY
The Crisp Sandwich

Yours Sincerely (please vote for me),
Gareth Horsepipe
MP for Purley North & Purley King
Houses of Parliament, London

PS. I've just noticed that you're six years old and can't vote anyway, so I don't care about your stupid packet of flippin' crisps.

You see. Not very helpful, and really quite rude. He suggested I get on to the Consumer Association, or a 'Which?'. I looked into these suggestions and found out the following:

1) 'Which' isn't how you spell 'witch'.
2) According to most scientists, witches don't exist.

There is a magazine called *Which?* that is printed by the Consumer Association, but they're the Consumer Association, not the Consumers-of-Crisps-Association, so what good is that to me?! Mark my words, if I wasn't going to stay six years old for ever, because I'm a cartoon, when I *was* old enough I would *not* vote for him!

Anyway, all this meant I found out that there is NO governing body to protect the rights of crisp eaters in this country, and there's no magazine or website that reviews crisps, corn snacks or nibbles of any sort.

So I thought *THINGS MUST CHANGE* (I thought it very loud) and so I created... *The London Review of Crisps!* (Purley Edition).

THE SNIFF TEST:

This is best done when you open the packet, and the crisps' chemical flavourings are at their strongest. Pull the sealed packet open and thrust your nose (if you've got one) deep in the bag sniff deeply. NB: With stronger, flavoured crisps, like Prawn Cocktail and Worcestershire Sauce, this may cause you to pass out. Do not be alarmed by this, but also do not do this whilst riding your bike, or operating heavy machinery. You can also sniff your crisps individually as you take them out of the packet, and before you eat them. Don't do this on the bus though, people tend to move away from you and mutter things about you under their breath.

THE LICK TEST:

Some stronger-tasting crisps can make you pull faces you didn't mean to pull and make you shout involuntarily if you put the whole thing in your mouth at once. Rather like testing a chilli's hotness, simply dabbing the end of your tongue on the most flavoured part of a stronger-tasting crisp can give you an idea of their taste/prepare you for the ordeal you're about to go through.

THE JUST EAT THE FLIPPING THING TEST:

Eat it and see what it tastes like.

SPIT?

Now, you'll have to do this with some flavoured crisps (Cheese and Onion! Yuck!) whether you mean to or not, but some crisp tasters do it on purpose! They're usually tasters who are sensitive to artificial colourings and flavourings and who have a funny turn if they eat too much artificial flavouring and colouring (I once threw an armchair at Barry Chuckle after eating half a bowlful of Skips). I'd only recommend spitting a chewed crisp out if you're tasting a whole mega-family pack that might put you into a salt/barbecue-rib-flavouring-induced coma.

Crisps of the World

In America crisps are called 'potato chips'! Crazy!

In Australia crisps are called 'chips'. But what do they call chips?! Hot chips of course.

Fan Mail!

Hello fans! Since going on telly we've, well, I've had loads of great fan mail from you fans about what great fans you are. So this section is my tribute to you, for being such great fans, and for helping me fill another couple of pages of this book. Give yourselves a pat on the back! But don't expect to be paid.

Dear MOTHER dear.

Just a note to say thanks for your help baking flans for the Purley Ladies' Flan Festival. Thanks to you we received a grand total of 14.501 flans. and 14.500 of those were yours!

Unfortunately they seemed to contain soap powder. so we've had to give all the money back. But the charity has been very under-standing about it. as they were when the same thing happened last year. and the fifteen years before that.

Thanks anyway dear.

Mrs J Medford.
Executive Chief Organising Lady.
The Purley Ladies' Flan Festival

- On **Wed, 7/28/10, MaxiWhoosh Fan Company <maxiwhoosh@maxiwhoosh.com>** wrote:

From: MaxiWhoosh Fan Company <maxiwhoosh@maxiwhoosh.com>
To: Big Howard <bighowardoliverdrinkwaterread115@bighowardoliver-drinkwaterread.rogernet.co.uk>

Mr BHOD Read,

Thank you for ordering an adjustable high-velocity MaxiWhoosh oscillating pedestal tilt fan with innovative room-cooling breeze technology. It is in the post.

Yours,
The MaxiWhoosh Fan Company

The MaxiWhoosh Fan Company does not accept liability for any lies told by any of its employees regarding whether or not things are in the post.

Erm, MOTHER, this is 'fan mail', not 'flan mail'. Our readers don't care about flans.

Oh for goodness, sakes. It's not THAT sort of fan mail, _Big_ Howard. Surely we must have some proper fan mail?

Dear Little Howard
pleaee could you
send me your auto-
graph as I am
your biggeet Fan...
oh hang on...-
Ah! That's better. Sorry I
had the pen in the wrong
hand. Anyway as I was
saying, I'm a tremendous
fan of yours. All the best,
Kevin Baxter,
rhyl. aged 42

Dear Little Howard,
I have been a big fan of yours for
many years. Please could you send me
an autographed picture of your face?
Also I am extremely interested oo
know what ies your favourite odour,
what is MOTHER's maiden name, and
what are your bank details? Also
where do you live, and when do you think
your house will be empty in the next
few weeks?
Yours, 'Daylight' Rob Berry

Roger T. Pigeon
Variety Artistes

DEAR ROGER t. PIGEON,
WHY OH WHY O Y O Y O Y don't you
HAVE YOUR OWN tV SHOW?
It's obvious to ANYONE
tHat you are tHe best And the
coolest And the best-looking.
AND the others are RUBBISH.
ActuAlLY YOU SHOULD PRESENT
TOP GEAR < (THAT WOULD be
GREAT!)
LotS o' love,
or... ROdNEY t. SEAGULL?

29

We've properly run out of ideas now, but *Big Howard* has just remembered that he ran a fan art competition recently and we could just bung them in! And THAT gave Roger an idea. He's dressing up as an artist and is going to do something on the next pages too!

Here are your pictures of me and *Big Howard!*

ROGER'S ART CLUB

HELLO! ROGER T. PIGEON HERE.

NOT A LOT OF PEOPLE KNOW THIS, BUT AS WELL AS BEING A HUGELY SUCCESSFUL AND MUCH-FEARED THEATRICAL AGENT, I AM ALSO A VERY ACCOMPLISHED PAINTER. AS A CHICK, MY PARENTS KEPT MY ARTWORK ON THE FRIDGE FOR YEARS AND YEARS, AND I LIKE TO THINK IT WASN'T JUST BECAUSE IT WAS COVERING UP A STAIN BUT BECAUSE I CREATE ART THAT LASTS. IN LATER LIFE, WHEN I HAD FLOWN THE NEST, I EXHIBITED MY WORK ALL OVER THE SHOP. UNTIL THE SHOPKEEPER CAUGHT ME. IN RECENT YEARS I HAVE MAINLY FOCUSED ON THE MEDIUM OF THE BACK OF PUBLIC TOILET DOORS. ANYWAY, WE'VE SEEN SOME OF YOUR DRAWINGS OF LITTLE HOWARD, BUT NOT ALL OF YOU HAVE DONE ONE, HAVE YOU, YA LAZY BEGGARS. SO HERE IS YOUR CHANCE!

THERE'S SOME PICTURES OF LITTLE HOWARD ON THE NEXT PAGE.
GO ON - COPY THEM.

33

ROGER T. PIGEON   AVERY COURT   PURLEY

* *

WRIT

* *

FROM: ROGER T. PIGEON

TO: ALL OF YOU LOT!

By the power vested in my vest I, Roger T. Pigeon, who is of sound mind and fine fettle, do sue you, the reader, for breach of copyright of the image of Little Howard, who I own TOTALLY, and that is backed up by the LAW and two whopping great gorillas behind me called Gus and Francine (his mother was an odd one).

I reckon that you did, on purpose, with no remorse, and with mallet of forethought, copy the image of one Little Howard, so that you could sell it to buy sweets or something on whatever day it was you got to this page of the book.

To stop me getting the fuzz involved send me a shed load of cash in a used, unmarked bag, for my attention, at my gaff. No funny business or Francine here will peel you like a 'narna.

Signed,

ROGER t. PIGEON

FEB 21 REC'D

35

Littlehoward.co.uk

'THE HOME OF ALL THINGS LITTLE HOWARDY!'

News flap!

New Book out!

New Film

About Little Howard
Little Howard Live
Things to watch
Press
Abour Howard Read
New! **Blog**
New! **Games!**
Contact
Brand New!  **Shop**

New!

* Little Howard Shop!

* Tour Dates! + trailers!

* New 'Big Question' Service

Visit the site for:

• Little Howard Games!
• Merchandise!
• Little Howard's own blog!
• Tour Dates – when Big Howard and Little Howard's live theatre show is touring near you!
• Exclusive clips and films
• Behind-the-scenes pictures and gossip from Little Howard's Big Question!

Dear reader with plenty of cash lying around,
(if this doesn't describe you then just skip to the next page)

If you're enjoying Little Howard's Big Book then ~~why not give us more of your money?~~ buy our other hugely successful book! !!!!

'Little Howard's Unpleasant Lullaby' was written by me, Big Howard before we were on telly, for a much younger age group than watch our show, so we've got LOADS of them left! Seriously, LOADS.

It's a picturebook lullaby about all the terrible things that happen to children if they don't GO TO BED RIGHT NOW! So it's a perfect gift for new parents, or little brothers and sisters you don't like.

LITTLE HOWARD'S UNPLEASANT LULLABY: GET THEM QUICK, BEFORE THEY'RE PULPED!

Little Howard's Unpleasant Lullaby

AS SEEN ON CBBC

AN OFFICIAL LITTLE HOWARD BOOK

NOT SUITABLE FOR...
WARNING!
...GROWN-UPS

Howard Read

When I was young, I mean obviously I'm still young. I'm twenty-three. But when I was ~~younger~~ even younger they had books called *Choose Your Own Adventure!* These were stories where you made decisions about what to do next, and it affected the way you died! They were brilliant, so I thought I'd nick the idea.

Here is my *Decide Your Own Adventure* story! It's a bit shorter than the originals, but then kids' attention spans have shrunk since I was a kid. I watched a documentary about it… well, most of one, I switched over after a while.

Anyway, I figure this will fill up a couple of pages and be the BIGGEST THRILL OF YOUR YOUNG LIVES!

Big Howard's

DECIDE YOUR OWN ADVENTURE STORY!

No. 1

You are Pegshift the Bog Elf. You live in a bog and you stink of old potatoes.

Go to No. 2.

No. 2

One day, you are sitting in your bog when a messenger whelk arrives. It arrives very slowly, because it is a whelk, and you don't notice it for several days. Then you do notice it!

WHAT WILL YOU DO?! YOU DECIDE!

Do you read the message the whelk brings or not?
Read the whelk's message — Go to No. 43.
Don't read the whelk's message — Go to No. 36.

No. 3

You tell the whelk that you will help him on his quest to rescue the lady bear. The whelk seems moody and grumpy with you. His attitude suggests that maybe you should have said you'd help straight away. What will you do?

Rishin' Rashin' Grumble Grumble...

YOU DECIDE!

Do you do what the whelk asks anyway, in spite of him appearing quite ungrateful? — Go to No. 4.
Challenge the whelk to a duel! — Go to No. 30.

No. 4

You jump astride the messenger whelk and tell him to take you to the lady bear in distress.

He doesn't like it much, but he carries you for a bit before getting tired. You have a rest, then you set off again. It's taking ages. Do you ...

YOU DECIDE!

Carry on trying to ride the whelk? — Go to No. 31.
Try to find a quicker way of getting to the lady bear? — Go to No. 11.

No. 5

You walk down the windy path towards the rickety cottage. Suddenly a strange creature jumps out of the bushes in front of you. Its head and face are those of a wolf, and its bum and legs are those of a slightly overweight cat with very fluffy fur!

It's a cat-werewolf! It snarls at you, bearing its teeth, and then cleans itself in a bad place with its tongue. You now have two reasons not to want to end up in its mouth. Eurch! It dives at your throat and you fall, flailing under its weight! What do you do?

YOU DECIDE!

Give up and let the cat-werewolf eat you — Go to No. 38.
Fight the cat-werewolf off, so it can't eat you — Go to No. 44.

No. 6

You walk down the windy path towards the rickety cottage. The whelk is now sliming into your ear and poking you with a little lance-like thing that comes out of his shell. He's really getting on your nerves. Suddenly a strange creature jumps out of the bushes in front of you. Its head and face are those of a wolf, and its bum and legs are those of a slightly overweight cat with very fluffy fur! It's a cat-werewolf! It snarls at you, and then licks its own bottom. What do you do?

YOU DECIDE!

Give up and let the cat-werewolf eat you — Go to No. 37.
Fight the cat-werewolf off, so it can't eat you — Go to No. 45.

No. 11

You decide to find a quicker way of getting to the lady bear — but how?!

YOU DECIDE!

Do you try to get loads of flying insects to carry you to the lady bear? — Go to No. 32.
Do you decide to carry the whelk? — Go to No. 33.

No. 12

You walk down the road towards the castle. It's MILES away, you get very bored, and you're a bit worried that there won't be any obstacles or adventures between here and the castle because the person who's writing this has run out of ideas.

YOU DECIDE!

Do you?
Go back to the tumbledown cottage (I would if I were you, it really doesn't look like there's anything up ahead) — Go to No. 21.
See if you can find a dragon and lob some rocks at it — Go to No 26.
Go and have a look at that MASSIVE SWAN over there — Go to No 29.

No. 13

You ask the massive bee politely if you can squeeze past and go into the SECRET PASSAGEWAY TO THE CASTLE. It seems quite engrossed in its knitting, so you can squeeze past quite easily. When you get inside you find that it is a secret passageway to the castle!

You enter the courtyard and hear a beautiful, gravelly voice echoing sweet songs down from one of the highest turrets! It must be the lovely lady bear princess!
You think about her longingly.

You climb the stairs, and reach a closed door, you try the handle, and it opens!!!
.... Oh good grief!

It turns out the bear isn't really your type. Do you —

YOU DECIDE!

Rescue her anyway — Go to No. 42.
Don't rescue her, but go home instead — Go to No. 24.

No. 20

You approach the tumbledown cottage. It looks rubbish. Are you going to go in, because I wouldn't. Seriously, rubbish.

What are you going to do?

YOU DECIDE!

Go into the rubbish tumbledown cottage? — Go to No. 46. Don't go into the rubbish tumbledown cottage? — Go to No. 12.

No. 21

You approach the tumbledown cottage. It looks rubbish (but trust me it isn't). I mean it looks rubbish, but looks can be deceiving can't they. And when you get in there be nice to the bee. I not trying to bring this to an end as quickly as possible, honestly I'm not, but seriously, be nice to the bee.

What are you going to do?

YOU DECIDE!

Go into the rubbish tumbledown cottage? — Go to No. 46. Don't go into the rubbish tumbledown cottage? — Go to No. 12 (where I happen to know you've already been — PICK THE OTHER OPTION OR WE'LL BE HERE ALL DAY)

No. 24

You decide to leave the lady bear, because, well, it's not her, it's you. You don't feel you're ready to commit to a relationship at the moment, especially not a potentially complex relationship like a bog elf/massive bear one. You back out politely but, clearly upset by your rudeness, the lady bear eats you.

THE END.

No. 25

Wait a minute! Why does it go from number 13 straight to number 20! And on the last page it jumped from number 6 to number 11!

You return to the tumbledown cottage, thank goodness. Go to No. 20. You won't regret it, the other way was RUBBISH.

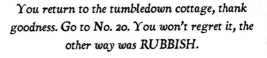

You try organizing a Choose — I mean *Decide Your Own Adventure* book. It messes with your head. If I'd used all the numbers I'd never have finished it! Just ignore it and carry on reading.

41

No. 26

You find a dragon and lob a rock at it. Before the rock even hits the dragon it has incinerated you with one snort of its fiery breath. Idiot.

THE END.

No. 29

You are attacked and eaten by the massive swan. And you know what, I think you did it on purpose.

THE END.

No. 30

You have decided to fight the whelk! You dive into the weapons puddle of your bog and pull out your fighting freshwater shrimp. It is very old, and you haven't used it for ages. Some of its legs are missing. You thrash at the whelk with it and it shifts from side to side. You imagine that's what whelks do if they're TERRIFIED. Then the whelk rises up and you see it has a nasty-looking lance thing. It's a dog whelk! And as everybody knows they can kill limpets by using their lance thing to inject shell-dissolving enzymes into their shells so they can slowly eat them!

Your fighting shrimp is rubbish, and bog elves have very slow reflexes so you are killed and eaten by what is basically a badly armed water snail.

THE END.

No. 31

You are attacked by a massive swan. It kills you. As your arm is being broken by a single blow of its wing for the twentieth time you realize that there was no way you could have predicted this happening. This only makes the whole thing worse.

THE END.

No. 32

You jump off the whelk and run to a clearing in the forest that you are in, but which I may not have previously mentioned. You call out your special bog elf call, which calls all insects that can hear your call to your aid.

One ant and a dragon fly turn up.

That's really not going to cut it. With a heavy heart you set off alone, as you notice that the whelk has been eaten by a massive swan. Go to No 34.

No. 33

You put the whelk on your back and it suckers onto you and crawls onto your head. You set off on foot to find the lady bear. Go to No. 35.

No. 34

You exit the forest. There is no whelk on your head, and before you lies an enormous, long valley, at the other end of which is a tall, wonky and mysterious castle! Surely this is where the lady bear is being held captive? What are you going to do?

YOU DECIDE!

Head down the valley to have a look at that swan down there? – Go to No. 40.
Head down the left-hand side of the valley where you can see a tumbledown cottage? – Go to No. 5.

No. 35

You exit the forest, with the whelk on your head, and see before you an enormous, long valley, at the other end of which is a tall, wonky and mysterious castle! Surely this is where the lady bear is being held captive? The mucus from the whelk's sticky foot is causing you some skin irritation. What are you going to do?

YOU DECIDE!

Take the whelk off your head and let it go? – Go to No. 48.
Head down the valley to have a look at that swan down there? – Go to No. 41.
Head down the left-hand side of the valley where you can see a tumbledown cottage?
– Go to No. 6.

No. 36

Seriously?
You're seriously not going to read the message?

YOU DECIDE!

Yes, seriously – Go to No. 50.
No, on second thoughts I will read the whelk's message – Go to No. 43.

No. 37

You just lie there and the cat-werewolf eats you. Even the cat-werewolf finds this a bit confusing and takes longer to eat you because it's a bit worried it's a trap. But it isn't, and it eats you and you're dead. The whelk crawls off, fat lot of good he was!

THE END.

No. 38

You just lie there and the cat-werewolf eats you. Even the cat-werewolf finds this a bit confusing and takes longer to eat you because it's a bit worried it's a trap. But it isn't.

THE END.

You are dead. To fill in a Customer Satisfaction Survey for this Decide your own Adventure Book go to No. 51.

No. 39

You start to really have a go at the massive bee's knitting. You say that its stitches are all uneven, and he should be using angora wool, instead of that tat. You tell the massive bee that it hasn't allowed for shrinkage, and that whatever it's knitting isn't going to fit whatever poor soul it's meant for after a couple of washes. The bee kills you.

THE END.

You are dead. To fill in a Customer satisfaction Survey for this Decide your Own Adventure Book go to No. 51

No. 40

You walk down the valley to the swan, as you get closer you realize it isn't a normal swan, but a MASSIVE swan that is further away than you expected! Go to No. 47.

No. 41

You walk down the valley, with a whelk on your head, to the swan. As you get closer you realize it isn't a normal swan, but a MASSIVE swan that is further away than you expected! The whelk jumps off your head and runs away. For some reason this doesn't make you stop going towards the massive swan. Go to No. 31.

No. 42

You leave with the lady bear, you come up against no resistance because the author is a bit bored and wants to get onto drawing some pictures of superheroes. There is a dragon, but it's got very poor hearing, and can only see in monochrome, you get past it EASY. It might also be that it was a plot by the bear to find herself a man, and that she was never in any trouble at all. Her and the whelk seem very chummy, I reckon the bear might have put the whelk up to it — you decide. Seriously, I don't know, it's up to you.

THE END – PS. YOU WON!

No. 43

You open the message, it is a plea for help from a really scared bear who is trapped in a very tall castle in a far-off kingdom called Goggarog. The bear is a lady! You are a boy (I hadn't mentioned that had I?)

YOU DECIDE!

Do you follow the whelk and rush to the aid of the lady bear? — Go to No.4.
Do you decide not to follow the message's bidding and get on with your life?
— Go to No. 49.

No. 44

You try to fight the cat-werewolf, but it is too strong! Well, its front half is, its back half is kinda cute and fluffy. You waste time stroking the nice fluffy ginger cat's tail, as the front half of the cat-werewolf eats you. As you die, you remember something you learned at bog elf school, and that's the only thing that can kill a cat-werewolf is a dog-whelk! You really are cross with yourself as you kark it.

THE END.

No. 46

You enter the tumbledown shack. In the corner you see an enormous bee. That's a bit weird, you think to yourself. The bee is doing some knitting, and it doesn't look like it's going to bother you, behind it you see what looks like a SECRET PASSAGEWAY TO THE CASTLE!

Do you:

YOU DECIDE!

Politely get past the bee and into the SECRET PASSAGEWAY TO THE CASTLE!? — Go to No. 13.
Criticize the bee's knitting — Go to No. 39.
Leave, because you're scared of bees, and you think that the SECRET PASSAGEWAY TO THE CASTLE is some sort of trap or dead end — Go to No. 31.

No. 45

You try to fight the cat-werewolf, but it is too strong! Well, its front half is, its back half is kinda cute and fluffy. You waste time stroking the nice fluffy ginger cat's tail. It looks like he's going to eat you. You hurriedly try to write a last will and testament with one hand while holding off its gnashing jaws with the other. Suddenly the cat-werewolf rises up in pain. You see, to your amazement, that the whelk is on the cat-werewolf's back jabbing at it with some sort of lance that is coming out of its shell. It must be a dog-whelk! They've got little lances that they use to attack barnacles haven't they!? And they clearly use them to attack their mortal enemies cat-werewolves, although this has never been documented in nature!

With a mournful howl, and a scratch behind the ear with its hind legs, the cat-werewolf falls to the ground and dies — dead! Thank goodness you didn't get rid of the whelk!

The dog-whelk eats the cat-werewolf by dissolving it with its spit and sucking it up through its hollow lance. It's revolting. You would have had a bit yourself but watching the whelk eat makes you feel a bit sick. You put a leg in your bag for later, and set off towards the rickety tumbledown cottage.

There's that swan again. Do you want to have a look at it on the way to the tumbledown cottage?

YOU DECIDE!

Go and have a look at the swan — Go to No. 40.
Go straight to the tumbledown cottage, you remember that you don't like swans — Go to No. 20.

No. 47

You are attacked by a massive Swan. It breaks your arm with a single blow of its wing, in the same place, over and over again. As you lapse from consciousness you think 'that's just showing off'.

THE END.

No. 48

You turn back into the forest and pull the whelk off your head. It turns around and is really quite rude to you. It has never spoken before and you are alarmed that it knows such filthy language. You turn back towards the valley as the whelk grumbles to itself resentfully. Go to No. 34.

Rishin' Rashin' Grumble Grumble...

No. 49

You decide not to do what the whelk's message says. The whelk follows you around for ages, nudging you and generally being a pest. What will you do?

YOU DECIDE!

Do you change your mind and rush to the aid of the lady bear? – Go to No. 3.
Do you decide to slay the irritating whelk because he's getting on your wick? – Go to No. 30.

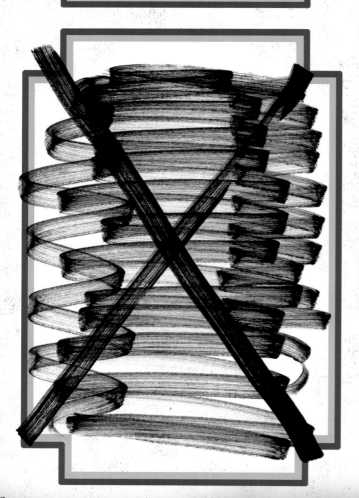

No. 50

You don't read the whelk's message, and so you don't even know anything about the quest, or the other bits of the plot. You spend the rest of your life in your bog and are ecstatically happy.

But in later life you have a nagging feeling you should have done more with your life.

THE END!

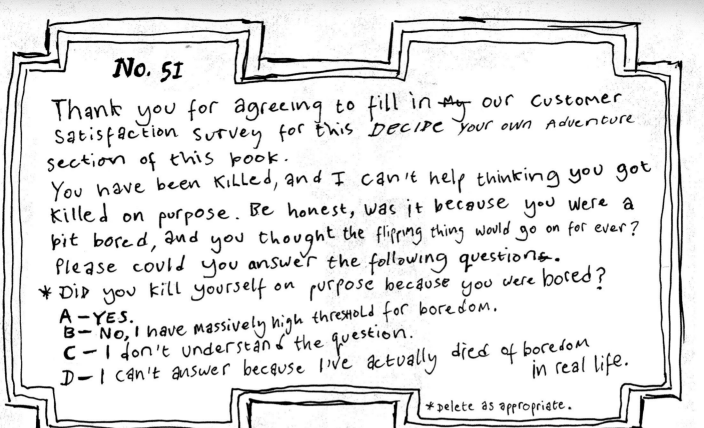

No. 51

Thank you for agreeing to fill in ~~my~~ our customer satisfaction survey for this DECIDE your own Adventure section of this book.

You have been killed, and I can't help thinking you got killed on purpose. Be honest, was it because you were a bit bored, and you thought the flipping thing would go on for ever? Please could you answer the following questions.

* Did you kill yourself on purpose because you were bored?

A — YES.
B — No, I have massively high threshold for boredom.
C — I don't understand the question.
D — I can't answer because I've actually died of boredom in real life.

*delete as appropriate.

Advertisement

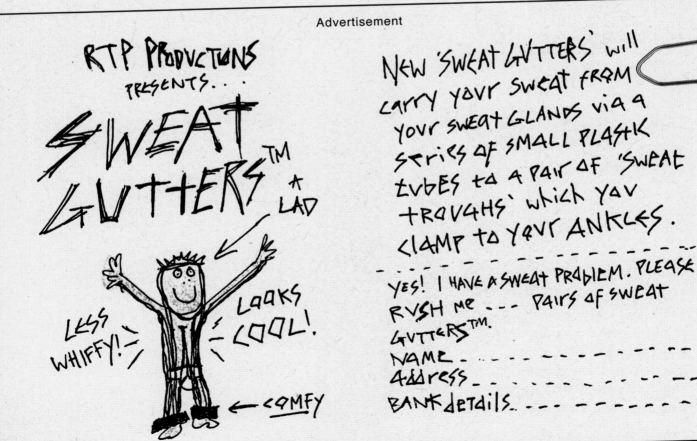

RTP PRODUCTIONS PRESENTS...

SWEAT GUTTERS™

↖ A LAD

LESS WHIFFY!

LOOKS COOL!

← COMFY

NEW 'SWEAT GUTTERS' will carry your sweat from your sweat glands via a series of small plastic tubes to a pair of 'sweat troughs' which you clamp to your ankles.

YES! I HAVE A SWEAT PROBLEM. PLEASE RUSH ME --- PAIRS OF SWEAT GUTTERS™.
NAME.
ADDRESS.
BANK DETAILS.

WORTHY WORD SEARCH

```
B O R I N G W E E R A M P 6 M O N K E Y
S H P O O P Y U K O B U M S A P E S S S
W I L L Y P L O P S H Y L O C K E D M B
B O T T O M B U R P S U S C B O D S A I
F P A N T S O N O E O C XL K E E P C L G
B U T T H O C K S R O K XXL S T I L L V H
N I C K E R S 3 P O O P E R H E E E O O
S C H A L L E N G E C L E O P A A O L W
K I N G L E A R Y 0 F A N T O N S P I A
K Y O T O B Y G U F F P R O S P E R O R
B U M C L E E O P P A T R B U M L O V D
L I T T L E H O W A R D O Y B O G M E S
U Y M Y Y M P D U C T S G B E L G E N M
N M O R O N A B F L S E E E E E E O T E
T U T R U T T I A E E J U L I E T E S L
B G H O W A R D S L O V E S C H E R E E L
O P E G G Y A G S P L A T H L U N C H S
Y O R E N O T N A A R I C H A R D I I I
D O D R W H O I F T C L E O P A T R A C
O W N T H E S W F R A F I D D L E E E EK
```

Hello. Big Howard here. I've asked Little Howard to put together an educational word search as part of the puzzle pages. I suggested characters from Shakespeare. I do hope he's done it properly.

WORDS TO FIND

Othello Prospero Toby Belch
Shylock Malvolio Antony
Bottom Coriolanus Cleopatra
Hal Romeo Falstaff
King Lear Juliet Richard III

Cross! Words

I've designed a *Cross!* Words of all the words I use when I'm cross. It's like a normal crossword, but the words are much better and each entry is followed by an exclamation mark.

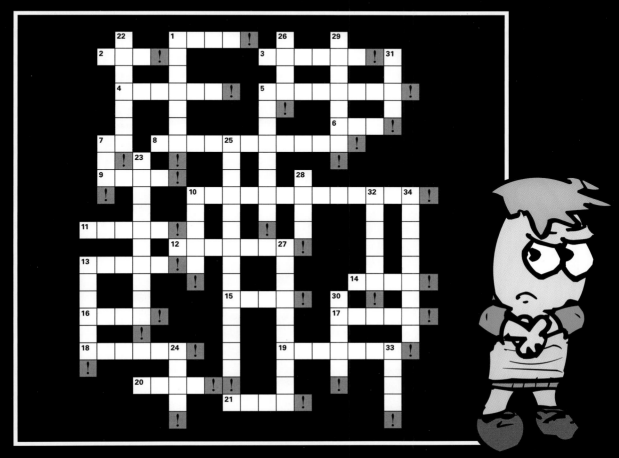

Across

1 What you say when you hurt your toe (4)
2 A short word for 'bottom' (3)
3 Saying 'no' in very, very, very slow motion (6)
4 To pester someone, sounds a bit like your sister, who's a boy (6)
5 What is he doing to that pancake? (8)
6 Saying 'no' in slow motion, but not very slow (3)
7 Word you say when you realise that something's gone wrong (2)
8 Another way of saying 'Silly Object' (6, 5)
9 If you don't believe someone you say 'my ----!' (4)
10 Don't ever return! (5, 4, 4)
11 What they call you if you're grumpy all the time (5)
12 When you really, really, really don't like something (6)
13 Be quietly very, very cross (5)
14 '---- stupid idiot!!!!' (4)
15 What big groups of people do when they are very cross (4)
16 Fool, idiot, wally (4)
17 Another word for 'cross' (5)
18 Annoyed. Sounds like the poltergeist off the Harry Potter books (6)
19 Another way of saying 'this *always* happens!' (7)
20 'You great big stupid ---- of horse poo!' (4)
21 Something you call someone you don't like (4)

Down

1 Telling someone to score a goal in football (2, 5)
5 What Roger says when he mucks something up, the fluffy bits on a bird (7)
7 What you say when you get a football in the goolies (3)
10 Another way of saying 'Under No Circumstances' (2, 3)
13 A rude way of telling someone to be quiet (4, 2)
22 You keep this in a bin (7)
23 Telling someone not to do something (4, 2, 4)
24 An old fashioned word for idiot, sounds like bolt (4)
25 '- ---- ----- ---- so angry' (1, 4, 5, 4)
26 When someone does something naughty in football (4)
27 Telling someone not to do something again (4, 2, 4)
28 Call someone an idiot, or trick them (4)
29 How you tell someone that they smell (3, 4)
30 What you tend to do if someone is really cross with you (5)
31 Very, very angry (4)
32 What you say if you're turning into the Incredible Hulk (6)
33 What you call someone if you think they're not telling the truth (4)
34 What they do on a police show on the telly when they lose someone in a chase (4, 1, 4)

*** See last page for answers ***

Little Howard's

Can you help Little Howard find his way through the maze to his Big Question Klaxon?

a-mazingly hard maze

A: No. Neither can we! It's flippin' impossible. I've run three pencils down to the nib trying to work out how to get through, but I keep going round and round in circles. I've even tried starting at the end, which I know is cheating, but I still can't do it. It's either the hardest, most fiendish maze ever invented, or it's just flippin' impossible. But they wouldn't print a maze that you couldn't complete in a book would they? That would just be pointless. Anyway, I'm going to have another go, see if it's third-day-of-trying lucky. If you can't be bothered to try again then that's fine with me. Seriously it's fine. Go on without me. Can I borrow your pencil though? Mine's run out.

PICTURE ①

PICTURE ②

SPOT THE DIFFERENCE!

Can you spot the difference between these two photos?

ANSWERS:

1. Little Howard is smiling in picture 2, but is not smiling in picture 1.
2. Little Howard has slightly longer hair in picture 2.
3. There is a rectangle of light in the top right-hand corner of picture 2, but the top right-hand corner of picture 2 is dark.
4. In picture 1 Little Howard isn't wearing his trademark yellow tank top, but in picture 2, he is.
5. In picture 1 no one blinked when the photo was taken.
6. Little Howard's hand is waving in picture 1, but not in picture 2.
7. Little Howard has long sleeves in picture 1, but short sleeves in picture 2.
8. Little Howard's hair is sticking up in the front in picture 1, but it is sticking down at the front in picture 2.
9. Pig Howard is wearing a snorkel in picture 1, but not in picture 2.
10. Pig Howard is wearing a snorkel in picture 1, but not in picture 2.
11. Little Howard is wearing a diving mask in picture 1, and not in picture 2.
12. Little Howard is wearing a diving mask in picture 1, but not in picture 2.
13. Little Howard is wearing a wetsuit in picture 1, but not in picture 2.
14. Pig Howard is wearing a wet suit in picture 1, but not in picture 2.
15. Pig Howard has wrinkles on his forehead in picture 1, but not in picture 2.
16. Pig Howard isn't in picture 2, but he is in picture 1.
17. Directly over Little Howard's right shoulder in picture 2 is Rick surface of the sea. Directly over Little Howard's right shoulder in picture 1 is a blob of light on the
18. Rick Parfitt from Status Quo has a striped jacket on in picture 2, but Rick Parfitt from the old-people's rock band Status Quo.
19. The background is mainly blue in picture 1, but it is black in picture 2.
20. Picture 1 is wider than picture 2.

21. There is a light shining over Rick Parfitt from Status Quo's right shoulder in picture 2, but Rick Parfitt from Status Quo isn't in picture 1.
22. Francis Rossi and Rick Parfitt from Status Quo are clearly sucking in their tummies in picture 2. Francis Rossi and Rick Parfitt from Status Quo aren't in picture 1.
23. No one has their thumbs in their belt loops in picture 1.
24. Picture 1 depicts two people going snorkelling, whereas picture 2 depicts someone meeting the two front men from four-chorded wonder-band Status Quo.
25. Picture 1 is underwater, and picture 2 isn't underwater, unless Little Howard and Status Quo are very good at holding their breath.
26. Picture 1 is a lot better framed than picture 2, the people are balanced left and right. There is a great big gap to the left of the people standing in picture 2.
27. Little Howard is with two people he greatly admires in picture 2. He is with Pig Howard in picture 1.
28. Francis Rossi from elderly gentleman's guitar band Status Quo has a looped earring in his left ear in picture 2. Francis Rossi from Status Quo isn't in picture 1.
29. There is a light shining over Rick Parfitt from Status Quo's left shoulder in picture 2, but Rick Parfitt from Status Quo isn't in picture 1.
30. Picture 1 is taken underwater. Picture 2 is taken in some sort of TV studio.
31. Francis Rossi and Rick Parfitt from the rock band-for-the-elderly Status Quo are not in picture 1, but they are in picture 2.
32. There are wires hanging from the ceiling in picture 2, but there aren't any wires hanging from the ceiling in picture 1.
33. There isn't a ceiling in picture 1, but there is in picture 2.
34. Rick Parfitt is wearing a white shirt in picture 2. Nobody, including Rick Parfitt, is wearing a white shirt in picture 1.
35. No one in picture 1 can play the guitar.

JOIN THE DOTS!

This is the HARDEST join the dots ever! It's so hard, I couldn't even do it when I was drawing it originally!!! So it hasn't turned out quite like I wanted. Good luck! If you can't do it, the answer is upside down at the bottom.

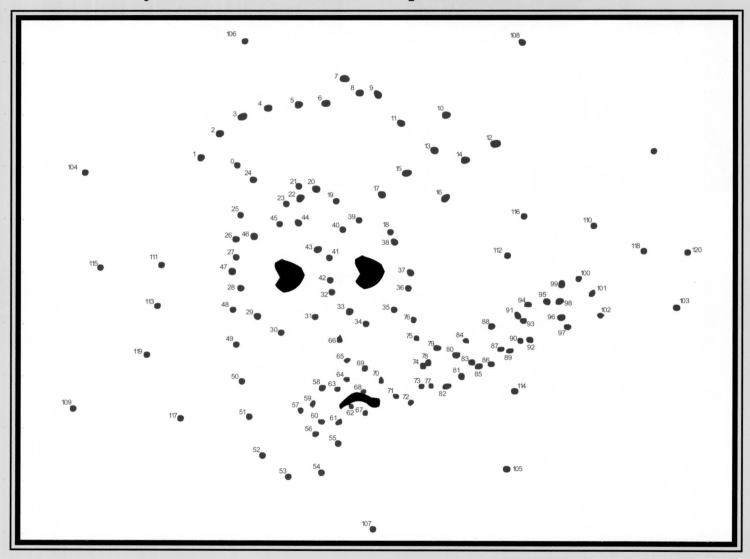

3.

2.

1.

ANSWERS: (In three stages, because it's tricky!)

54

CORRECT THE GAGS!

OH NO! Big and Little Howard's secret joke book has accidentally been shredded by a ravenous badger. They've rescued some tatty scraps, but they need help putting the jokes back together! Can YOU tell which parts of which joke go together? Or do you think they're funnier as they are?!

1 DOCTOR DOCTOR, I FEEL LIKE A PAIR OF CURTAINS!

A DON'T TALK TOO LOUD, EVERYONE WILL WANT ONE!

2 WHAT DO YOU CALL A DEER WITH NO EYES?

B CLIFF.

3 WHAT DO YOU SAY TO A DEAF GORILLA?

PULL YOURSELF TOGETHER! **C**

4 WHAT'S BLACK AND WHITE AND RED ALL OVER?

A WOOLLY JUMPER! **D**

5 WAITER, THERE'S A FLY IN MY SOUP!

COCKER–POODLE–DOO! **E**

6 WHAT DO YOU CALL A MAN WITH A SEAGULL ON HIS HEAD?

ANYTHING YOU LIKE, HE CAN'T ~~HERE~~ HEAR YOU! **F**

7 DOCTOR DOCTOR, I THINK I'M GOING TO DIE!

NO, IT'S JUST THE WAY I'M STANDING. **G**

8 WHAT DO YOU GET IF YOU CROSS A SHEEP WITH A KANGAROO?

NO-EYED DEER! **H**

9 WHAT'S GREEN AND GOES UP AND DOWN?

HUMPHREY. **I**

10 WHAT DO YOU GET IF YOU GET IF YOU CROSS A COCKER SPANIEL WITH A POODLE AND A ROOSTER?

DON'T BE SILLY—THAT'S THE LAST THING YOU'LL DO! **J**

11 WAITER, DO YOU HAVE FROG'S LEGS?

OINKMENT! **K**

12 WHAT DO YOU CALL A CAMEL WITH A FLAT BACK?

A GOOSEBERRY IN A LIFT! **L**

13 WHAT'S BROWN AND STICKY?

A PENGUIN IN A BLENDER! **M**

14 WHAT DO YOU GIVE A PIG WITH A RASH?

A STICK. **N**

Answers: 1G, 2H, 3F, 4M, 5A, 6B, 7J, 8D, 9I, 10E, 11G, 12I, 13N, 14K.

55

Little Howard's
DREAMY DREAMWORLD OF DREAMS!

STOP THIEF!

Dreams. Dreammmms? Dreeeeeams! What are they? Are they really weird TV programmes beamed into your brain when you sleep by a satellite in space controlled by psychic aliens?* Or are they messages from the future which warn us about things that are about to happen?*

So I thought I'd write down some of the things you might dream about and then tell you what they mean.

* <u>NO</u> – BH

BEING NAKED IN CLASS

If you dream that you are naked in class, it means you obviously really want to be naked in class. This is perfectly normal, so don't worry. Next time it happens just have fun with it. However, DO NOT actually do it in real life. It's always chillier than you'd think.

BIG HOWARD

If you dream about Big Howard – of trying to run away from him but not being able to move, or that he's sitting on top of you and squashing you into the sofa with his massive bottom – it may mean that you live and work with him all the time, every minute of every day, forever. This is not a good omen.

CYCLOPS

Dreaming of a Cyclops might mean that you are too narrowly focused on one thing at the moment, and maybe you should be more open-minded. Dreaming of a Cyclops dressed in a short skirt, stockings and high heels, however, might mean you are a bit too open-minded.

DINOSAURS FIGHTING SPACE ALIENS

If you dream about dinosaurs fighting space aliens, it may be because you've been thinking a lot about dinosaurs fighting space aliens, or drawing pictures of them, or watching a film in which dinosaurs fight space aliens. This is perfectly normal. Usually it means you will continue to think about dinosaurs fighting space aliens, and who'd win.

DOING A WEE

If you dream that you are doing a wee, often it signifies that you really are doing a wee. Do watch out for that.

DREAMING

I once dreamt that I was in bed, asleep, dreaming that I was in bed, asleep, dreaming that I was in bed, asleep, dreaming that I was in bed, asleep, dreaming that I was in bed, asleep, dreaming that I was in bed, asleep, dreaming that I was in bed, asleep. This normally means you should wake up.

HOME

The home that you have in a dream is not necessarily your 'dream home'. Sometimes I dream that I live at the bottom of an empty crisp tube in a wheelie bin with a very big-headed donkey. That is not, however, the 'house of my dreams'. You see?

KISSING LITTLE SUSAN

If you dream of kissing Little Susan, it usually indicates that you will be very embarrassed around her the next day, and will have to avoid talking to her for a while.

NOTHING

If you dream of nothing, it signifies that you are very lazy. Honestly, you can't even be bothered to dream? The rest of us are in there, fighting off wombats and getting naked in class, and you're just lying there grunting out of an empty head. Make an effort.

PIGEONS

If you dream of fat greedy northern pigeons, you are probably about to lose a great deal of money.

RING-TAILED LEMUR STEALING YOUR FAVOURITE PLATE

If you dream that a ring-tailed lemur is stealing your favourite plate, it could mean that you are going to have a brioche, and then get the bus to the library. Well that's what happened to me after I had that dream.

THE QUEEN

If you dream of the Queen it might mean you've been keen to be seen to be clean and green on screen, not to preen your spleen in the routine teen canteen scene. But it probably doesn't.

US FINISHING THIS BOOK ON TIME

Yeah, dream on.

Little Howard's Song Lyrics

NEVER TRUST A PIGEON

LITTLE HOWARD:
Never trust a pigeon with your money or career,
If you lend him anything, it's sure to disappear,
Pigeons should be viewed with suspicion, dread and fear,
Never trust a pigeon.

Some of them are scrawny, some of them are fat,
I'd only trust a pigeon on the inside of a cat,
They are what you get if you stick feathers on a bat,
Never trust a pigeon.

[Phone rings.]

ROGER:
Surely all pigeons can't be that bad,
It's just a bad experience that you have had.
I know I nicked some money but let's not go mad,
There's nothing wrong with pigeons.

LITTLE HOWARD:
Pigeons are nasty, pigeons are sly,
They are what you get if you stick feathers on a fly,
You ask Nelson's Column and he'll reply
Never trust a pigeon.

[Phone rings again.]

ROGER:
We are just misunderstood,
In our pigeon chests we're good.
Be you stool pigeon or wood,
You can always trust a pigeon.

BIG HOWARD:
Who are we are we to hand him our damnation
Maybe it's because he's animation!
Never trust cartoons!

LITTLE HOWARD:
You can't say that! That's appalling,
There are so many things that you're ignoring.
I'm not like him, just because I'm a drawing!
There's nothing wrong with cartoons!

BIG HOWARD:
It's not fair, that's my point.
Don't get your beak all out of joint.
You can't judge people by what they look like,
We can't judge you by another cartoon tyke.

LITTLE HOWARD:
Yes, ok, I think I see.
If I judge him, then he can judge me.
But on one things we can agree.

BOTH:
He's a mean mean pigeon.
He's a mean mean pigeon.
He's a mean mean pigeon.
He's a mean mean pigeon.
He's a mean mean pigeon.
He's a mean mean pigeon.

Pigeon! Pigeon! Pigeon! Pigeon!

ROGER: No I'm not!

LOVE'S A GREAT BIG MOTORBIKE

BIG HOWARD:
Love.
Love's a little bit like like,
But like's a stroll, and love's a hike.
Like's a tricycle and love's a great big motorbike.

And love,
Love's a little like a crush.
But that's a nudge and love's a push.
Crush is a sapling
And love's a great big holly bush.

Yes love.
Love's a little bit like care,
Just there's a lot more of it there.
Care is a guinea pig and love's a great big grizzly bear.

CHORUS:
Love's when you mean it in capital letters,
Written in red and underlined,
Love makes you bigger and bolder and better,
Love is a feeling that cannot be defined.

VERSE:
But love.
Love's a little bit like like,
But like's a stroll, and love's a hike.
Like's a tricycle and love's a great big motorbike.

And love,
Love's a little like a crush.
But that's a nudge and love's a push.
Crush is a sapling and love's a great big holly bush.

Yes love.
Love's a little bit like care,
But there's a lot more of it there.
Care is a guinea pig and love's a great big grizzly bear.

But motorbikes crash,
And holly will scratch,
And grizzly bears tear you apart.
Love is a feeling that nothing can match.
But love's the only thing will break your heart.

The Lord Fortiscue Squilp

Franky

Goodnight From Him

The Classic

Now I'm not saying you have to stick these on Big Howard, but they are here if you want them.....

Shakespeare

Ginger Chops

Chaplin

Groucho

The Geography Teacher

Place Head Here

Rabbit Ears

Teeth and Tongue

Full-on Santa

HUNKY HOWARD 'BIG HOWARD' READ OFF OF TV'S LITTLE HOWARD'S BIG QUESTION

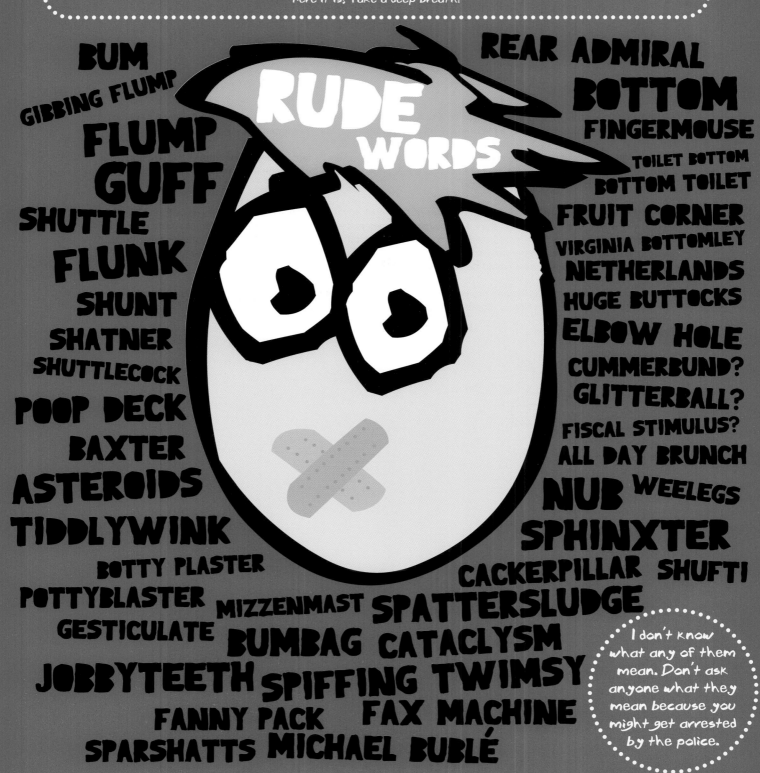

For some reason, most adults refuse to use rude words in front of children, which is a terrible shame because rude words are the words most self-respecting children really want to learn.

Some grown-ups do use rude words in front of children, but by a strange quirk of fate, nearly all grown-ups who use rude words in front of kids are REALLY SCARY. Even though they're using rude words that I really want to hear, I also really want to slowly back away out of the room and never come back.

As a public service to you, dear reader, I would like to tell you ALL THE RUDE WORDS I KNOW. I do this because you are my fans. And because I want you to know what they mean, so you can be really impressed when I slip them into conversation, and this book. The other reason I want to tell you these, is to fill some space in this book.

Here it is: Take a deep breath!

RUDE WORDS

BUM
GIBBING FLUMP
FLUMP
GUFF
SHUTTLE
FLUNK
SHUNT
SHATNER
SHUTTLECOCK
POOP DECK
BAXTER
ASTEROIDS
TIDDLYWINK
BOTTY PLASTER
POTTYBLASTER
GESTICULATE
JOBBYTEETH
FANNY PACK
SPARSHATTS

REAR ADMIRAL
BOTTOM
FINGERMOUSE
TOILET BOTTOM
BOTTOM TOILET
FRUIT CORNER
VIRGINIA BOTTOMLEY
NETHERLANDS
HUGE BUTTOCKS
ELBOW HOLE
CUMMERBUND?
GLITTERBALL?
FISCAL STIMULUS?
ALL DAY BRUNCH
NUB WEELEGS
SPHINXTER
CACKERPILLAR SHUFTI
MIZZENMAST SPATTERSLUDGE
BUMBAG CATACLYSM
SPIFFING TWIMSY
FAX MACHINE
MICHAEL BUBLÉ

I don't know what any of them mean. Don't ask anyone what they mean because you might get arrested by the police.

Another Note From the Publisher

Dear Reader,

If you've made it this far into the book you're a better man/woman/boy/girl than I am. You're definitely a better girl. I make a rubbish girl. I look like a pig dressed up as a Barbie, but that's not important now.

I am doing my very best to try to make this book as good as possible. I am. After my last letter I got arrested for a short while and only released if I promised to make this book readable by the time it got printed. But that's in a couple of days now, and look at it! It's nonsense!

The other morning we had a meeting and neither of them had any ideas worth printing. Little Howard said his favourite word was whelk, and so why don't they do a couple of pages just with the word WHELK written over and over again in different fonts. Then Big Howard said you could only do that if you followed it up by putting one massive WHELK! across a two-page spread, maybe over a picture of a whelk. I had to tell them that if they did that their supply of doughnuts in their writing room would be stopped.

Needless to say, I'm very sorry, and no, you still can't have your money back. I'm hoping that by the end of the book I'll be able to claw some sort of order together. Wish me luck.

Scott

Scott Pack
Publisher
The Friday Project

The Friday Project . HarperCollins Publishers . 77-85 Fulham Palace Road . London . W6 8JB

www.thefridayproject.co.uk

LITTLE HOWARD'S BIGFEST!

June 7, Aug 15, Oct 4 in Our Back Garden

BANDS ON THE BILL SO FAR :

Three days of peace, love and music and hopefully a giant hog roast too!

THE LITTLE HOWARD BIG BAND

LITTLE HOWARD
vocals /guitar/ lyrics/ recorder / bongo/ banjo/ klaxon

* BIG HOWARD
triangle

* MOTHER
keyboard

* ROGER
merch

SUSANS ALOUD

surprisingly loud.

Boy band down the Swings

special one-off performance NOT by the swings...

Uncle Roy & the Rubbish Magicians

will they turn up, or is this another of Uncle Roy's wind-ups?

DJ JAZZY JETMAN UK

New project for the failed jet-pack inventor. This won't get off the ground either.

very little harvey's floppy blue blues

smooth, mellow, flopped-out vibes from the stuffed legend

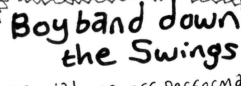

TICKETS COST £190.00 MAKE SURE YOU GIVE IT TO ROGER T. PIGEON PRODUCTIONS

Working Title: 'The Big Splash'

BH

LH

Fig I.

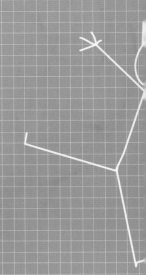

Fig 2.

Fig 4.

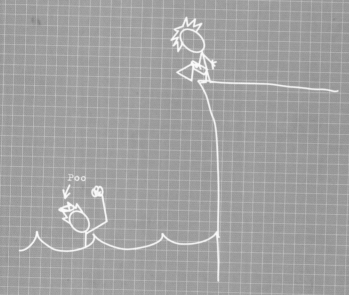

Poo

Working Title: 'Splatwich'

Fig I.

BH

Butter knife

LH

Jam

JAM

Bread on plate

Working Title: 'Fly Away'

BH dressed as a fly
for fancy-dress party

LH

Fig 2.

Fig I.

Fig 1.

Fig 4.

Fig 2.

Rhinoceros

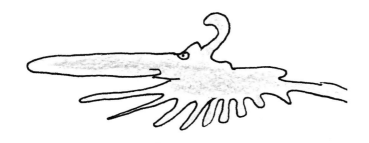

BIBBLEDY FLAP-NUBBLER

A squetchy and bibbledous Willthisdonimal with long tubble-dunks for bim-hundling its ouchspreen and flibbyflabbing and so on.

JELLIMUNGAZOID!

Jellimungazoid! lives in the freezer and comes out during parties where he always snaffles the buffet when nobody's looking.

THE WRIKIJAVOOZ

The Wrikijavooz cackles when embarrassed (which is all the time!) and emits empty bubbles when its head is inside itself! (which is nearly all the time!)

BARRELHEAD

Old Barrelhead has the head of a barrel. Which is to say, his head is shaped like a barrel. Yes indeedy-do. Decidedly barrel-headed, old Barrelhead's head.

SKOOBALOOBALOOB ST. MUKKLEDUKKEMUK

Erm...

Will this do?

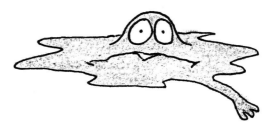

FLUBBO LUMMO

Flubbo is part-bump, part-puddle. He brings out the maternal instincts in young women, then steals their handbags.

THE BRAIN OF SCHNORBIUS

No idea, sorry.

....This won't do.

GLOBBLEROCKER

Globblerocker, aka Greasy Yellowfoot, is made entirely of engine oil and completed Guitar Hero with his eyes tied behind his back.

'4 NOSES' GUPTAL

Has four noses, one for each smell (Food, Flowers, Old Books and Nasty Business). Sneezing is a disaster.

ZIGVSKSWOOLO

Half his head is spiky, the other half smooth. Oh, and he lives down a hole.

CLONK

Only exists to remind me what time it is, and is currently reminding me this book should have been finished ages ago.

INVIZZY BUNKLIN

Never stays still long enough to be drawn! Which is lucky 'cos it's lunch time.

Clockwise from top:
Big Howard's Big Curry;
Roger T. Pigeon's Worm Kebabs;
MOTHER's Computernoffee Pie;
Little Howard's Big or Little Pizza

House Recipes

Big Howard has had a great idea! We'll all do our favourite recipes! Remember though –
if you're going to use the kitchen, whatever you do make sure you have an adult
present to wash up and tidy everything away.

BIG HOWARD'S BIG CURRY!

You will need:

- Some bits of meat
- A jar of nice sauce
- Rice

Get the meat and cook it up, then add the sauce. Make sure it's a nice sauce. Some people make their own sauce for curry but I say: Why bother? You can get sauce in jars these days. Meanwhile, cook the rice. And voila! A curry. Yummy!

LITTLE HOWARD'S BIG OR LITTLE PIZZA (SIZE IS OPTIONAL)

That didn't take up much space, Big Howard. This should make up for it. This is a classic recipe, and here's a very simple nineteen-point plan to help you get the best results. You will need:

- The number of a good pizza takeaway
- Some money

1) First, get a bit hungry.
2) Then think *What shall I eat?*
3) Then think *I know, pizza!!.*
4) Make your way towards the number of a good pizza takeaway and look at it.
5) Put the number into a telephone and ring it up.
6) Wait for someone to answer the phone.
7) When someone answers, MAKE SURE IT'S DEFINITELY A PIZZA TAKEAWAY. If it's a bowling alley or a florists or the World Health Organization, JUST HANG UP.
8) Ask them for a pizza.
9) Hang up.
10) Try and wait for the pizza. Maybe run around loads or jump up and down on the sofa shouting "PIZZAAA!!!"
11) After an hour, phone back and ask where the pizzas are.
12) Give them your address.
13) Wait for the pizza while looking out the window being really hungry and annoyed.
14) When the pizza arrives, use the Some Money to pay for it.
15) Open box.
16) Eat pizza.
17) That's it.
18) Sorted.
19) Hooray!

MOTHER'S COMPUTERNOFFEE PIE

Hello readers! MOTHER here. How lovely to be asked to share one of my favourite recipes with you all. I never write down any recipes, they're all up here in my memory banks, which are functioning perfectly. OK, some of them were damaged when I crashed last week, but I'm sure I can remember a simple recipe.

You will need:

- Some bananas
- More bananas
- Bananas
- 4 bananas
- 1 banana?
- A pie
- Toffees
- 17 toffees
- A jar of toffees?
- Bananas
- Banoffees?
- A computer

Right, erm, mix all the bananas with the toffees. Then... ooh, what happens next? Ah, er, sprinkle in some banana and toffee. Then... add the banoffees? No, wait, there's meant to be biscuits in this isn't there? Get some biscuits. Or is it cheese? No... .... hang on >>

Add more bananas. And toffees. Place under the toaster... or is it the fridge? Oh dear, sorry loves, it's been a while. Then add a computer. And there you have it... Stuffed olives? No... um... [rfkcjn <runtime error>

ROGER T. PIGEON'S WORM KEBABS

Right, listen up. Worm Kebab is a traditional Barnsley recipe which dates back to the late 1990s. First you need worms, second you need a skewer. Put the worms on the skewer. Then eat them.

For a bit of added nutrition you can always pop some fungus on the skewer, or some bogeys. Brown ones are better for you than green ones.

If you're still hungry after that, and I always am, why not nick a kiddie's chips?

LITTLE HOWARD'S

Brilliant

THE ONLY CAFÉ IN PURLEY STAFFED ENTIRELY BY 6-12 YEAR-OLD BOYS!

-Menu-

Firsts:

TOFFEE APPLE............£2.50

BEEFBURGER WITH SMARTIES IN...........1 HULK MASK

TUNA MAYO IN A BOWL...........3 BEN-10 CARDS

7 MICROWAVE MINI HOT DOGS............12 MILEY CYRUS PIX

Seconds:

PIZZA SANDWICHES............1 CATAPULT

EGGY BREAD WITH CHICKEN DRUMSTICKS............1 FIVER

TOFFEE APPLE.............£3

REALLY MASSIVE BOWL OF CEREAL..........1 SUPERBARIO DX GAME

Caff!

LITTLE HOWARD'S
BRILLIANT CAFF,
12a CHUNDERFORD CUTTINGS,
PURLEY

*Don't book ahead, the boy
on the phone is useless*

*The management respectfully
designates that mums,
sisters and Jamie
Olivers are not
permitted in this
restaurant.*

Thirds:

BIG PINT OF MILK WITH CHOCOLATE BICUITS CRUMBLED IN.........£1
FLYING SAUCER ATTACK!..................3 DANDY ANNUALS
MOTHER'S 'YUMMY' COMPUTER CAKES.........FREE
TOFFEE APPLE................£3.50

Fourths:

!?!...............I THINK YOU'VE HAD ENOUGH, MATE

Side Orders:

14 READY SALTED CRISPS..............1 K9 BADGE
GOBSTOPPERS............2 MARBLES (WE SHOULD CHANGE THIS—LH)
TOAST WITH CHOCOLATE SPREAD............DO A MOONIE OUT THE WINDOW
HUNDREDS AND THOUSANDS...........1P EACH*

* THIS WAS ROGER'S IDEA

Drinks:

CANS OF POP..............BRING YOUR OWN

79

ACTIVITIES!

Why Not Try Being ...

A VAMPIRE!

By Your Vampiring Correspondent

LEEETLE NOVAD (Mwa-ha-ha-haaa!)

If you're stuck for something to do on rainy afternoon, or if you run out of things to do during a school holiday, why not try becoming a vampire?! I'll tell you why not, because it's RUBBISH!

Being a vampire looks all glamorous on *Buffet the Vampire Slayer*, *Twiglet*, or *Sesame Street*, but in reality it's very boring.

I think the problem might be that I'm really a day person, and vampires really have to be *night* people, because if they go outside to play in the garden or down the park during the day, they'll get evaporated to ashes by the sun.

The problem is I, like most six-year-olds, get up quite early and go to bed at about half past seven, so it's very hard to adjust to a life (or after-life) of night stalking. If I go out of routine I get REALLY CRANKY. You don't see many vampires on *Twiglet* having a tantrum at the bottom of the stairs because the DVD player didn't record *The Tweenies* (which is most vampire's favourite programme.) Secondly, spending all day in a box is very dull and quite uncomfortable. I don't

have a proper coffin, so I use the box that my mini golf set came in instead.

Vampires in the films just lie there staring at the ceiling all day, but I tried that and it gives me energy-legs. What do you do all day if you're a vampire? I don't know if you're allowed to watch telly. The problem is that lots of TV shows on during the day have sunlight on them, and I don't know if you get dissolved if you just see sunlight on telly. So I don't know if I should be dissolving into ashes when I watch Big Howard's *Complete Home and Away* box set.

HERE ARE SOME IN-COFFIN ACTIVITIES I'VE COME UP WITH:

1. VAMPIRE I-SPY.

This works by putting on a Count Dracula voice and playing I-Spy like 'I! Count Dracoool spy viz mine leetle eye, zee top of the inside of a cardboard box!... Mwah-ha-ha-haaa!' That sort of thing. It's hard to play this for long if you don't have anything very interesting to spy on the inside of your box.

2. GUFFING.

This is obviously worth doing whether you're pretending to be a vampire or not, but make sure you've got some air holes punched in your coffin. If you're a proper actual vampire you don't have to do this because proper actual vampires cannot be killed by guffs (except garlic guffs)!

3. READING BOOKS.

But what ever you do *don't* read *Dracula* by Bram Stoker because, in spite of being the book that made vampires popular, it is RUBBISH. There are loads of really long bits about people reading each other's diaries, and about a girl being a bit poorly and lots of people asking to marry her. It gets good when the bloke who eats flies arrives. That's as far as I've got.

4. NAPPING.

Surely that's allowed.

I get hungry lying in my box all day. But if you're a vampire all you can eat is people's blood! It's a very strict diet and two things you DEFINITELY CAN'T EAT are garlic (I know! Not even in mini chicken kievs!) or steak, because steaks can cause heart disease in vampires.

Getting human blood is almost impossible, especially if your friends and family are like Big Howard and won't let you have any of theirs. I tried giving blood at the doctors, (which is tricky if you're trying to be a night-stalker, because they close at five o'clock!). I went to a blood-

doning session and asked if they did a buy-back service, but apparently they don't, and I'm too young to give blood anyway!

The solution I came up with for day-time blood-drinking is to drink Ribena instead. But an all-Ribena diet, even Ribena Toothkind, is a lot of sugar which is not good news if you're planning to spend your whole day lying still in a box.

Give Blood
here
(No Under 18s)
(No Vampires Except Guide Vampires)

Once you have successfully spent the day lying in your coffin and the sun has gone down it is TIME FOR VAMPIRES TO COME OUT AND PLAY! I rise, slowly out of my coffin, go 'Mwah-ha-ha-haa!' and creep around the house to find poor helpless victims to feed on. I'm not allowed to go out of the house on my own after dark though, so it's mainly Big Howard I have to stalk after. I don't know if you've noticed, but Big Howard can be quite grumpy, and he generally likes to go to bed at night, and SLEEP apparently. I've found that he doesn't like being pounced on by a blood-thirsty vampire very much.

So I end up sitting on the sofa with the telly on and by half past eight I've usually fallen asleep!

IF YOU'RE THINKING ABOUT BECOMING A VAMPIRE, PROBABLY DON'T BOTHER. I CAN'T SEE WHY PEOPLE TAKE IT UP.

Song Lyrics

WILL THE DINOSAURS EVER COME BACK?

BIG HOWARD
Will I ever chat to,
A velociraptor?
Go one-on-one,
With an iguanodon?

Will my eyes alight on,
An anatotitan?
Will they ever focus,
On a diplodocus.

BIG HOWARD
Oh will I see a t-rex attack?
A stegosaurus's spikey back?
Utahraptors hunting in packs?
Will the dinosaurs ever come back?

LITTLE HOWARD
Will I share my packed meal,
With a pterodactyl?
Will I give my coleslaw,
To an ischiasaurus?
Give my fizzy pop,
To triceratops?
'Please have a slice of cheese,
Saurornithoides'

BIG HOWARD
(spoken)
Sing the chorus to a brontosaurus!

BIG HOWARD
Oh will I see a t-rex attack?
A stegosaurus's spikey back?
Utahraptors hunting in packs?
Oh will the dinosaurs ever come back?

LITTLE HOWARD
But a stegosaurus,
is gonna floor us.
And a pterodactyl,
Would have me for a packed meal.
With an iguanodon,
I'd get stepped upon!
A tyrannosaurus,
is gonna want to gore us.

BOTH
I hope the dinosaurs don't come back,
Or else I'll be a t-rex's snack,
I've seen a brontosaurus attack,
I hope the dinosaurs don't come back.

I hope the dinosaurs don't come back,
Or else I'll be a t-rex's snack,
I've seen a brontosaurus attack,
I hope the dinosaurs never come back.

A DINNER FOR DODOS

BERT
(sung)
I like to give you the best there is,
But I don't have the staff.
So if a dog is sick on my vest,
I wipe it off with my scarf!

BIG HOWARD
It's a tea time for toilets,
It's dinner for dunnies,
It's a lunch that your loo will like,

LITTLE HOWARD
But it's not good for tummies.

BERT
(sung)
I want to give you the very best,
That's what no one understands,
So when I go to the gentlemen's,
I don't have time to wash my hands!

BIG HOWARD
It's a dinner for dodos,

LITTLE HOWARD
(confidentially)
It's not good for your doo doos,

BERT
Please try one of my doughnuts,

BIG HOWARD
It will just go straight through you.

LITTLE HOWARD
(in the style of a flamenco singer)
Ayyy ay ay ay ay ay,
Ayyy ay ay ay ay ay,
Ayyy ay ay ay ay ay,
Ayyy ay ay ay ay ay,

Ayyy ay ay ay ay ay,
Ayyy ay ay ay ay ay,
Ayyy ay ay ay ay ay,
feel sick.

BERT
(sung)
My food is very greasy,
But you'll lose weight through diarrhoea.
If you try my dysentery,
You'll practically disappear!

BIG HOWARD
It's a tea time to die for,
It's a supper for suckers,
It's a dinner to do you in,

BERT
But it's a breakfast for truckers.

ALL
It's a supper to die for,
It's a dinner to do you in,
It's a lunch that your loo will like,

BIG HOWARD
At Bert's Greasy Caff Inn!

LITTLE HOWARD
At Bert's Greasy Caff Inn!

BERT
At Bert's Greasy Caff Inn!

BRILLIANT!
MAGAZINE

ISSUE 01 – 8 AUGUST 2010

ONLY
£8.76
RRP
(RECOMMENDED ROGER PRICE)

WILL TV'S BIG HOWARD FINALLY REVEAL WHAT'S IN HIS SECRET SHED?

EXCLUSIVE!
ROGER T. PIGEON INVITES US TO HIS FIFTH VERY CHEAP AND QUICK WEDDING

'I'M VERY MUCH IN LOVE WITH... SORRY DEAR, WHAT'S YOUR NAME AGAIN?'

Big Howard's...
Secret Shed

An Expozay by Little Howard

Big Howard reading his 'fan mail' looking flattered.

Big Howard beaming and posing like Prince William in a palatial apartment.

Big Howard with his 'very dangerous' garden shears.

When I, Little Howard, asked Big Howard if I could do a big exclusive article about his shed, with pics, for my own brilliant magazine, *Brilliant!* Magazine, his first reply was, 'No. Mind your own business, nosy!'

This wasn't very nice as I don't have a nose and I can get a little sensitive about it so I stormed off in a huff. Later on he apologized, so I asked him again but he still refused. Then I said we'd had lots of fan mail asking about the shed, that all his fans really wanted to know all about it, and that it was in the public interest to let me have a look in it. This time he agreed!

Of course there wasn't any fan mail, I wrote it all myself, but my brilliant plan had worked. At last! I could see inside Big Howard's shed!

Only problem was... it was really boring. Just an old garden chair, a bike, a stepladder, a lawnmower, a tool kit, some plant pots and a bag of charcoal briquettes. But by this point I'd already promised him the front page, I'd crossed my heart and everything, so I had to pretend to be interested.

What, I wondered, inspired him to put the plant pots on the garden chair?

'That was mainly because there was no other place to put them,' Big Howard replied, fascinatingly. 'But I put the bag of charcoal up against the bike deliberately so it wouldn't fall over.'

Nice one. And why, as there's nothing very interesting in the shed at all, does he make such a fuss about me not going in there?

'You weren't allowed in because it's got dangerous things in it like these garden shears.'

As a grown-up, Big Howard spends most of his day worrying that if I found a pair of garden shears, I'd use them to cut bits of myself off, because he obviously thinks I'm a maniac.

'And besides, it's nice to have somewhere to come and relax sometimes.'

Well thank you Big Howard for letting *Brilliant!* Magazine look inside your extremely ordinary garden shed.

'Don't go yet! There's a pretty funny story about the stepladder... Come back!'

Roger's Shabby Wedding
By Little Howard

'She's definitely the one. It can't have been me, mine always smell of eggs.'

Roger T. Pigeon has been married four times before, but he reckons there's something special about Montserrat, the exotic cockatoo he married in a Bolton registry office in a bit of a hurry last week.

'She's very brightly coloured, I like that,' said the happy pigeon, biting the wedding rice out of his feathers.

But is it love? 'Oh yeah. Whatever love means!'

Well, I think it means the powerful feeling of attachment and affection and excitement that you feel about someone who you want to spend the rest of your life with.

'Oh! In that case, no,' Roger decided, tucking more wedding fruit pellets under his wing for later.

And what about the new Mrs T. Pigeon? Why did she marry Roger? Why?

'Chirrup chirrup, tweet tweet, £500, twitter-woo, UK citizenship… squawk,' she says in between whacking great beakfuls of wedding seedcake. She is tropical, so doesn't know much English.

'We never argue about anything,' Roger announces to the press (= me). 'Mainly because neither of us understands what the other one is saying. Makes it hard to disagree.'

Big Howard's...
'My kind of day'

MORNING! THE BEST PART OF THE DAY!

I like to get up at 6am, so I can clang around the kitchen loudly or stand outside Little Howard's bedroom door tutting and muttering that he hasn't got up yet. If it's a weekend I do the same but say 'you're wasting the best part of the day,' again and again and again as well. All adults like to do this and even we don't know why.

Sometimes I think Little Howard deserves a lie-in. On those days I just quietly get on with whatever I've got to do around the house. Usually this involves drilling into concrete or taking up, buying and then practicing the Tuba or Euphonium. If Little Howard is still in bed by half nine I sometimes start blowing up crates of iron girders in the back garden. This usually does the trick.

A HEARTY BREAKFAST!

They say breakfast is the most important meal of the day, so I like to make sure it tastes revolting and has the texture of something a donkey might sleep on. In America there has been a lot of research done. Loads of it. And they've concluded that the more deeply unpleasant your breakfast looks and tastes, the better it is for you. Because of this I like to have a breakfast of wholegrain silage-muesli, with lentil shavings, unwashed brown rice, and some grass clippings scattered on the top. On a weekend I might do myself a fried egg, then throw it away in disgust without eating it. This does make me really quite miserable, but research has shown that being miserable keeps you slim.

After my muesli-mulch I do some Yoga. Strawberry Yoga is my favourite.

DOWN TO WORK!

Like many high-flying media creatives I've got a home office. This is the only room in the house where I allow myself to wear a tie. I like being my own boss mainly because it gives me someone else to boss about! As a boss I'm very strict when it comes to DRESS CODE. So, before I get to my office I nip into the downstairs toilet to get changed or there will be HELL to pay to myself! I'm quite a demanding employer. I 'don't suffer fools gladly' (which means I shout a lot) and I 'speak my own mind' (which means I swear a lot — only at the office though because Little Howard just starts giggling uncontrollably when I use bad language).

My dress code is TIE AND PROPER (POLISHED) SHOES. For those who have never worn a tie, it's like a very thin bib, that's really expensive to wash, or replace if you drop food on it. It also reminds me where my goolies are if I ever forget, which is invaluable with my hectic schedule.

MY WORKING DAY

10.00am prompt. I sit down and answer my fan mail. I believe very strongly that us celebrities owe everything we have to our fans, and answering all of their letters and emails should be our number one priority. After all, she *does* write every single day, and without her, I wouldn't be here. I wouldn't have been born and I'd have to do my own washing.

At 10.05am I drop the replies to my fan mail off by hand, and usually have a cup of tea and a chat with my mum while I'm there.

LUNCH

They say that lunch is the most important meal of the day (this is a different 'they' to the ones that say breakfast is the most important meal of the day, there are fewer 'Theys' that say this, but does that make their opinion less important? No it doesn't). Because lunch is so important, and because I'm usually famished because I never eat much of my revolting breakfast, I usually have something deep fried for lunch, and some cake.

IT'S GYM TIME!

As a celebrity, it's important to keep myself in shape, and that shape is 'unthreateningly slightly podgy'. In the scripts to our shows we make it very clear that my character has a hint of a double chin, and a little bit of a belly. If I ever lost these vital character assets I would definitely have to sack myself. Maintaining just the right level of chubbiness is hugely important to my career so it's gym time! For a bit.

I spend two hours at the gym every day. Mainly for the sauna and the energy drinks.

IT'S TEA TIME!

A lot of people don't call tea 'tea', they call it 'dinner' or 'supper'. To make sure I don't get it wrong I have all three.

OH NO! I'VE FORGOTTEN TO WRITE ANY OF THE BOOK!!!

It's usually just after tea that our publisher, Scott, phones up and complains that I haven't sent him any pages of the book today. This is usually true, because, usually, I've completely forgotten, what with the Tuba practice, and the gym, and the eating. I spend the evening trying to think of great ideas for the book. Or I fall asleep after twenty minutes of trying to think up ideas, and only wake up when I fall off my chair.

Little Howard's...
'My kind of day'

1. Get up - whenever Big Howard makes me get up.

• •

2. Watch TV, muck about, set off klaxon.

• • • • • • • • • • • • • • • • • •

3. Go to bed, whenever Big Howard makes me go to bed.

YOUR HORRORSCOPES

WITH *Little Howard*

There are twelve signs of the zodiac. The zodiac is a massive roll of camera film in space and on it you can see these stars that if you join them up are pictures of fish and animals and things. Obviously you have to squint a bit, and fill quite a lot of the picture in yourself. Anyway, some people can tell what your week's going to be like just by looking at the zodiac (for ages)! People who can do this are called astro-lodgers, because they pay rent per week on the spare rooms of stars.

ARIES - The Hairy Ram

☆ ARIES ☆

(March 21 - April 20)

PEOPLE will continue to shout 'Hairy!' at you in the street this week, because you are all very hairy. All Aries people are descended from the Hairies, a tribe of people who were all mostly born in late March and April and were very hairy, like you.

Aries people are very 'assertive'. You fly off the handle on Monday, are very bossy on Tuesday and Thursday, and you go off in a huff on Wednesday. Oh, and you throw a strop on Friday afternoon.

Aries people are go-getters, so go-get knotted.

TAURUS - The Bully

☆ TAURUS ☆

(April 21 - May 21)

TAURUSES are very determined, stubborn and loyal, except the ones who aren't, and you all have very dirty hands. Go on, wash them again. Honestly. The other star signs are always waiting at the dinner table for Taurus to wash his hands properly. Come on Taurus, spit spot, the casserole's getting cold. Tsk.

The first ever thing born under the sign of Taurus was the stegotaurus, which was a herbivorous quadroped from the late Jurassic period who was very determined, stubborn and loyal.

In later life you will vote Conservative.

GEMINI - The Twits

☆ GEMINI ☆

(May 22 - June 21)

IT says on the Internet that Gemini people are very intelligent, but you're not because this week you're all going to be hit in the eye by a flying iced gem. Again! How'd you manage that, you numpty? Typical gem in eye.

CANCER - The Crab

☆ CANCER ☆

(June 22 - July 23)

YOU are a decapod crustacean whose abdomen is hidden under your thorax. You are covered with a thick exo-skeleton and have a pair of nasty claws. As if this wasn't bad enough, you are also a terminal disease. Frankly the zodiac would be better off without you. Although you do make quite a nice sandwich paste.

✦ LEO ✦

(July 24 - August 23)

LEO is a fire sign (No Naked Flames, that sort of thing) and is ruled by the Sun (I wouldn't let that newspaper tell me what to do if I were you). Also, all Leos are called Leo. Leo is the shortest of all the zodiac signs, and the only one spelt L-E-O. Don't know anything else about Leo, my telescope can't see it as it's over the other side of the flats.

LEO - The Lion With An Afro

✦ LIBRA ✦

(September 24 - October 23)

THIS week you will continue to work in a library, which is where all Librans work, even though you can't spell very well. You will also wee yourself again, because people born under the sign of Libra wee themselves all time. If you're a Libra and you don't wee yourself, don't complain to me, I didn't say it, this is what the stars say. Complain to them.

LIBRA - The Speak-Your-Weight Machine

✦ SAGITARIUS ✦

(November 23 - December 21)

A GOOD week for the Sadgitarian - you go straight to the top of your class after an accident in the chemistry lab! No, sorry, that was a joke. I can't see Sadguitarius 'cos the gasworks is in the way but it's definitely the hardest star sign to spell.

SADGITARYUS - The Archers

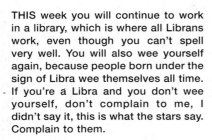

✦ AQUARIUS ✦

(January 21 - February 19)

YOU are a water sign which astrolologically means you are a great big drip (aaah haha). All Aquarians were born in aquariums, which is why you always make sure you shut your front door. This week Mars is in conjunction with Uranus, so watch out for that.

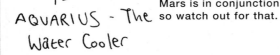

AQUARIUS - The Water Cooler

✦ VIRGO ✦

(August 24 - September 23)

YOU are a girl.

VIRGO - The Girl

✦ SCORPIO ✦

(October 24 - November 22)

YOU are a predatory arthropod with a big spiky venomous tail, and you also played in a 1970s German heavy metal band. Scorpions are the most powerful and self-obsessed and completely flaming bonkers of all the zodiacal signs. This week, people will try to avoid you, and only some of them will be lucky enough to manage it.

SCORPIO - The German Heavy Metal Arachnid

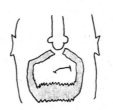

✦ CAPRICORN ✦

(December 22 - January 20)

YOU will drive a Ford Capri while eating corn – which is very dangerous. You will also meet a tall dark stranger but don't get too excited 'cos it turns out to be your shadow. You will come into money, but only about 20p.

CAPRICORN - The Goaty Beard

✦ PISCES ✦

(February 20 - March 20)

PISCEANS are emotional and creative, which is a nice way of saying you are all raving mad liars. Pisces is the wettest of the water signs, even soggier than Aquariuses, so you'll spend all week flapping about in a daze as usual. Look out for nets and worms on the end of hooks, Wetty McFishface.

PISCES - The Fish (and Chip Supper)

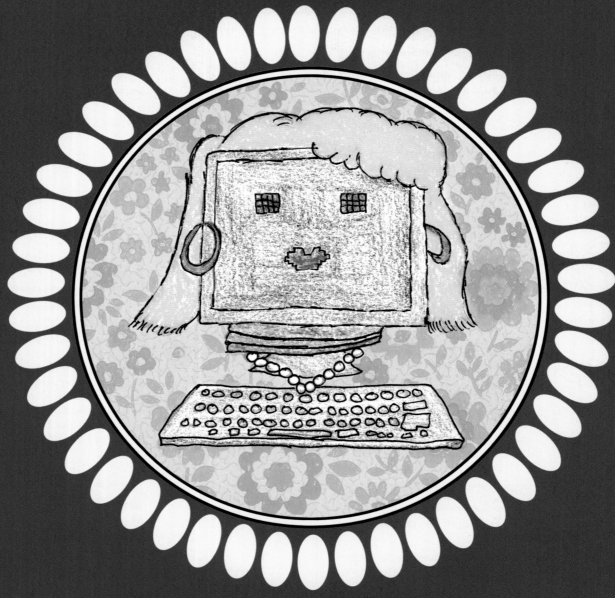

MOTHER
Knows Best...
Top advice on your deepest emotional problems and home computer niggles from our agony aunt who causes more agony than any aunt, MOTHER.

Dear MOTHER,
I was going out with this boy but he packed me in for my mate Donna and now I'm all confused. What sort of thing can I do to help with that?

Yours,
BooHooGrrl, Putney.

MOTHER SEZ: 'Simply select the negative emotions you wish to delete and drag them to the Trash basket on your desktop. Then, right-click on Trash and select Empty Trash. This should do the trick, unless you have a virus. In which case, phone MOTHER's Oh Dear Me So You've Got A Virus' Helpline.

Dear MOTHER,
I currently have a Pentellium InterSwish 5 (PCO 3.453 gHz), Compu70435 Motherboard, 1 gig DRD8 Rams, M PIXCOR 7H679002 (7866RPM) hard drive and a GeoWhiz4x 550 video card. I want to upgrade my video card to give me 1 gig outboard memory. Which video card should I upgrade to?

Yours,
Basically Looking To Upgrade My Video Card, Leicester.

MOTHER SEZ: 'Well, Basically, are you sure that's what you really want? Sounds like you're not trying hard enough to save your relationship with your current video card.

If you showed it some respect and attention maybe you'd find in time it will give you all the outboard memory you need. Keep at it.'

Dear MOTHER,
My home computer is convinced that it is my mother. Is there a program I can install which will make it understand that it isn't?

Yours,
Fed Up of Purley

MOTHER SEZ: 'You know full well she is your mother, you cruel man. Why do you have to say these things? After all she's done for you.'

Dear MOTHER,
I really am colossally smelly. I never have a bath, I eat very hot curries and I live in a nest full of my own droppings. I love it. But recently my foul stinking odour has been putting off potential business deals. So I need advice on how to remove someone's sense of smell without them noticing. It sounds drastic, but it really is the only way I can see that these people will overcome this problem.

Yours,
Roger T. Pigeo – er, actually no, someone else.

MOTHER SEZ: 'Have a wash, you filthy pest.'

BOY DOWN THE SWINGS

In our local park there's a boy who seems to know everything. No one knows where he's from, or even if he has ever left the general swings area, but he has agreed to share his wisdom with you, dear reader, in exchange for Big Howard's NASA flask and Jenny from round the corner's mobile number.

Hmm, I'm not sure I like you talking to this Boy Down the Swings, Little Howard. That all smells a bit fishy to me...

...And I want my NASA flask back!

How dare you! I'll have you know I wash daily.

BOY DOWN THE SWINGS, HE SAY...

- All candyfloss is made from old ladies' hair.
- All the girls in the world have a meeting every week to decide what's going to happen.
- The earliest trains were in fact horses dressed up.
- Nobody actually lives in Australia, everybody there is on holiday.
- Football was invented at Football School, in the town of Football, in the Midlands, when a boy dropped the rugby ball and started kicking it.
- The Internet smells of peppermint.
- My mate's dad invented DVDs.
- And he can sell you some if you want.
- In real life, none of the Mr Men really get on.
- Man hasn't actually walked on the moon – Neil Armstrong was in fact a remote-controlled robot.
- My brother's mobile phone can contact the dead. The day after our dog died he got a text that said 'woof'.
- Our dog could write and send text messages.
- Babies grow in the cabbage patch. I know this because I saw what my dad was doing in the allotment at lunchtime.
- The Queen technically owns every towel in the country.
- Chocolate is poisonous to little brothers.

DRAGONMOON:™

MagicMoonQuest™

Instructions

-- The Rules --

DragonMoon™: MagicMoonQuest™ is a swords-and-warlocks fantasy fight-type turn-based trading card game in which YOU have to work your way up from Apprentice Runebabbler to Mighty High Lord Chief Controller and Commander Over All Quadrants and Spheres – which is quite a task, I can tell you.

You have to buy a load of cards, because there are loads of different types of card. There are Weapon Cards, Friend Cards, Foe Cards, Terrain Cards, Spell Cards, Travel Cards, Non-Peak Travel Cards, all sorts of cards.

Say, for example, you start with this hand:

Runic Orbmaster IV
Habitat: Outskirts of the Blinking MoonDeep.
Questing Moonskills: Inflatable Stamina Pouch;
Weather-Mouse Control Guru; Keeper of the
Dragon's Napkins; Beardspells 12.
Flinging: Mid-high.
Conjuring Chant: 'Get on with it!'

✱ FRIEND CARD ✱

1️⃣ **FRIEND CARD: RODOMONTOGAAHL**
If you have the Friend Card Rodomontogaahl, it means you can throw a thirty-one-sided dice to determine how much a percentage of his Questing MoonSkills you can summon for assistance (assuming you're at a stage of the game with full Summoning Rights; if not you need to wait a bit). If you roll a square root, you have enough Summonation Power to summon that square root expressed as a percentage of Rodomontogaahl's Questing MoonSkill. Which means, for example, you will be able to use a fraction of his Inflatable Stamina Pouch, which is sort-of handy against certain Foe Cards.

THE DIV CUPBOARD

ENCLOSE FOES FOR 3 GOES

❋ WEAPON CARD ❋

② WEAPON CARD: THE DIV CUPBOARD

With this Weapon Card you can enclose your foes within the Div Cupboard for three goes. During this time:

They are not allowed Spellcasting Privileges

They are not allowed Summoning Rights

They are not allowed to go to the lavatory

Unless the Div Cupboard is counteracted by a Foe with an Enchanted Crowbar, in which case you put the card in the Rubbish Cards pile, which you then have to try and swapsie with someone who's only just started playing.

SHARDSPIRAL

Controlling Overthing: Maddamantax The Wizwitch.
- **2 Big Dark Woods**
- **168 Vulnerability Trees**
- **3 Unpredictable Troll Communities**
- **3 Bridges of Eternal Woe**
- **1 Smashing Little Shoe-shop Just off the High Street**

❋ TERRAIN CARD ❋

③ TERRAIN CARD: SHARDSPIRAL

A Terrain Card will magically transport you to the terrain on the card – that's easy enough. But in Shardspiral, for example, Summoning and Spellcasting are quite tricky because a lot of it is out of signal range. You may have to roll a spherical minus-dice to determine the percentage of the percentage of the Questing MoonSkill that you're trying to deploy. You are also more open to attack, and you daren't hide behind any of the Vulnerability Trees. In fact if you've got this Terrain Card then it's curtains for you (unless you have the Enchanted Crowbar, of course, and then you're laughing).

④ FOE CARD: BIMPSH

If you get this Foe Card, you've got nothing to worry about. Bimpsh may not even exist – there are a few stories about his ominous wisps and his unholy gobcasting, but mainly from people who've had too much of the old fungus tea. Even if he does exist, his Flinging is only Underlength, so if he casts a curse it'll probably miss you. Almost any Questing MoonSkill will banish him – unless you're in Shardspiral, which according to this hand you are, so you're pretty much doomed.

BIMPSH

Elfghost of the Rimchasm
Habitat: Tendrils Sweet Tendrils.
Questing Moonskills: Ominous Wisps; Tongue-lashing of Faerie Folk; Violet Flesh When Excited; Gobcasting.
Flinging: Underlength.
Conjuring Chant: 'Ouch!'

❋ FOE CARD ❋

KNOCK-TAPPING THE RENDLEJEAMS

WITH THIS CARD YOU CAN KNOCK-TAP ANY RENDLEJEAMS AT ANY TIME

❋ SPELL CARD ❋

⑤ SPELL CARD: KNOCK-TAPPING THE RENDLEJEAMS

Spell Cards give you instant access to a nice juicy Spell, with no need for dice-rolling or Summoning Rights. Unfortunately very few of the Spells seem to make any sense. So if you get this card, you can Knock-tap the Rendlejeams – but that might not be any help at all, because nobody knows what they are or what effect that has. Sometimes it becomes clear, but not often.

So, basically you'll pick it up. I have scattered some more of my own DragonMoon™: MagicMoonQuest™ cards over the next couple of pages because a) it helps to familiarize yourself with the sorts of Foes, Friends, Weapons and Terrains you might encounter if you start playing the game and b) we've still got loads of space to fill in this book.

GOOD LUCK, AND MERRY MAGICMOONQUESTING™!

DRAGONMOON:
MagicMoonQuest™

DRAGONMOON:
MagicMoonQuest™

HAPPY BIRTHDAY!!!

WISHING YOU MANY HAPPY RETURNS ON THE OCCASION OF YOUR BIRTHDAY

✳ BIRTHDAY CARD ✳

6 BIRTHDAY CARD
If you have a Birthday Card, you have to give it to one of your opponents' Friend Cards, with a little something you've gift-wrapped for them. Tread cautiously: if you buy a nice present, you may win the Friend Card off your opponent and bolster your allegiances (nice trick if you can do it!). But if you try and fob them off with a tatty old jumper, they may besiege your Terrain and send giant metal hawks to massacre your family. It's a minefield, it really is.

7 TERRAIN CARD: THE WASTES OF TIME
If you have two Terrain Cards in one hand, you have to roll an eighteen-legged dice to determine which Terrain you dwell in for this round. UNLESS you have the Wastes of Time card, in which case you are cursed to stalk the endless barren wastes, not just for the remainder of the game, but for the REST OF ETERNITY. You are not excused from play, you must be present at every game, but you cannot summon, enchant, travel, slay, protect, rebirth, hide, deploy, retreat, pass Go, collect £200, or do anything at all except stand there in silence as your friends carry on playing.

DRAGONMOON:
MagicMoonQuest™
MANUISK

Waiter of Quadrants
Habitat: *The Bistro Where All Life Began.*
Questing Moonskills: *Anticipating Cosmic Hiccups; Stardust Guffs; Triumphening the Metaskartch Using Only a Spoon.*
Flinging: *Wow!*
Conjuring Chant: *'Twazzagumbo Twazzoo... oh how does it go, erm...'*

✳ FRIEND CARD ✳

8 FRIEND CARD: MANUISK, WAITER OF QUADRANTS
Polite to a fault, Manuisk is a valuable Friend – the only problem is he has an accent which renders half of what he says totally illegible. His Spells sometimes don't work, but his Stardust Guffs have got to be seen to be believed – even then, you still won't believe the smell.

Well...this journey was a mistake!

✳ TERRAIN CARD ✳

MADDAMANTRAX

The Wizwitch of Shardspiral
Habitat: Two dry-heaves east of Bumbooga.
Questing Moonskills: The Fluxing of Nutterjank; Rebirthing (on Throne Squares only); Upskirt Exaltations; Natty Cardies.
Flinging: Through-hair.
Conjuring Chant: 'I am not a woman!'

✱ FOE CARD ✱

CLYTOR THE GLUCIENT

Oafwarrior Maximus
Habitat: The Wastes of Time.
Questing Moonskills: Colossal Death Capacity; Infinite Sarcasm; Firm Stare; Thorough Filching.
Flinging: Hard-up.
Conjuring Chant: 'Wooooaaarrrgghhh!'

✱ FOE CARD ✱

9 FOE CARD: MADDAMANTRAX

If you pick Maddamantrax for a Foe, you're for the high jump! Literally. Everyone who picks this card has to jump over a five-foot bar. It is hard to beat Maddamantrax, but it can be done – he is lactose intolerant. So all you need is a tin of squirty cream, or stick a few Mini-Milks in a catapult. And he hates it when you mistake him for a woman.

CRUMBLEBONCE

The Old Old Old Old Man
Habitat: He recently moved into a smaller one-level cave because the stairs in his old cave were getting a bit much.
Questing Moonskills: Sharp Tutting; Bemoaning the Wind; Snooze Power; Stick Brandishing; Horrid Cough.
Flinging: Meh.
Conjuring Chant: 'Bit wet out today.'

✱ FRIEND CARD ✱

10 FRIEND CARD: CRUMBLEBONCE

Dear old Crumblebonce. They say he's over a million years old, but he isn't, that's just cruel teenagers' gossip, he's actually about eighty-three. His great wisdom is legendary across the DragonMooniverse, but so is his damp, cabbagey smell.

11 FOE CARD: CLYTOR THE GLUCIENT

Clytor is a big old softie really, so if you pick him as a Foe you can get the better of him by showing him pictures of kittens in slippers and things like that. He is Rock Hard, but never got the hang of Arm Wrestling. He lives among the Wastes of Time, and can often be heard wandering around lamenting the lack of pubs.

Little Howard's Song Lyrics

YOUR EYES THEY CAN PLAY TRICKS ON YOU

UNCLE ROY
(Spoken over music)
Believing your eyes,
Is not always wise.
It sometimes defies belief.
So next time your eyes
Tries telling you lies
Be brutal, be frank and be brief.

BIG HOWARD
Your eyes can play tricks on you,
You can't always believe them.

LITTLE HOWARD
If they pop out you have to retrieve them
If they fall in dog poo you have to leave them.

BIG HOWARD
Your eyes can play tricks on you,
Things are not always what they seem,
Like a rainbow is just a wet sunbeam,

LITTLE HOWARD
And the thing about dog poo was actually a bad dream.

BIG HOWARD
Your eyes can play tricks on you,
It's all about perspective.
Or your mind being selective,

LITTLE HOWARD
Or your eyes are wonky so your glasses are corrective.

BIG HOWARD
Your eyes they can play tricks on you,
You've got to keep them in focus.
Please focus on this crocus,

LITTLE HOWARD
That's not a crocus, it's a camouflaged locust.

BIG HOWARD
Your eyes they can play tricks on you,
Is it real or just a drawing?

LITTLE HOWARD
Which one should we be ignoring,

BIG HOWARD
If everything was real then life would be boring.

FINALE (THINK VEGAS ELVIS)
But sometimes your eyes!
They try to deceive,
And you just have to ignore them,
And simply believe!
I believe I'm a man!

LITTLE HOWARD
I believe I'm a boy.
(Pulls out brioche)
And that this is an illegal use of my image!

UNCLE ROY
And that I'm Uncle Roy!

ALL
Because sometimes belief,
It is all that we've got!
You must believe in yourself!
Believe it or not!
Aaaaaaahhhh, AaAAAAAAHHhhh, Aaaaaaaah!

SLAP STICK!

LITTLE HOWARD
There are many different things that you can do in this old world,
Every life must find its own true path.
But please do take a moment as your fortunes are un-furled,
You could try to make somebody laugh!

BIG AND LITTLE HOWARD
Slap stick! Slap stick!

LITTLE HOWARD
You may not approve,
But it can make me laugh so hard
That I can hardly move!

BIG AND LITTLE HOWARD
Slap stick! Slap stick!

LITTLE HOWARD
You may not agree,
But you can't have seen a
Cartoon monkey fall out of a tree!

You can try out witty banter,
You can hit 'em with a pun,
You can shock them with the truth or with a lie.
You can dooble your entendre,
'Cos doing it is fun,
But if in doubt just hit them with a pie!

BIG AND LITTLE HOWARD
Slap stick! Slap stick!

LITTLE HOWARD
You may think it's coarse,
But you can't have seen a fat man,
Falling off a horse!

BIG HOWARD AND LITTLE HOWARD
Slap stick! Slap stick!

LITTLE HOWARD
You may think it's base,
And you will not be laughing,
When this pie goes in your face.

Give a man a fish
And he will eat for a day.
Teach him how to fish
He'll eat for life.
But if you hit him with a fish,
He just won't know what to say,
But you will really entertain his wife!

BIG HOWARD AND LITTLE HOWARD
Slap stick! Slap stick!

LITTLE HOWARD
You may not approve,
But it can make me laugh so hard
That I can hardly move!

BIG HOWARD AND LITTLE HOWARD
Slap stick! Slap stick!

LITTLE HOWARD
You may not agree,
But it can make me laugh so hard
I do a bit of wee.

LITTLE HOWARD'S

GUIDE TO THE

GALAXY

by *Little Howard*

Space. Spaaace. Spaaaaaaaace!! What is it? Where is it? And can you go there for your holidays?* Space is basically the sky after it gets dark - so when you look up at night and it's black and there are stars and a moon, that's space. But when it's blue and there are clouds, that's not space, that's just the sky. Um, the sky disappears at night and behind the sky is space, which goes back a very long way, or something like that.

Space is very dangerous because it's very dark, and there are aliens in it. The aliens probably have much more bigger better eyes than us, so they're all right, but we need special suits and torches and things like that. If you think you want to go into space, DON'T! A better idea is to sit at home with a doughnut and imagine what you <u>might</u> find up there. That's what I've done.

(Big Howard says my galaxy map isn't 'accurate', but has he ever been to space? No. Closest he's ever got is the loft.)

* No, of course you can't, don't be so silly.

'Solar doodles'

 h's hat (on)

 The Star

The Sun

 The Mirror

 Mars

 Fun-size Mars

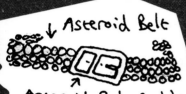 King-size Mars

 Flying saucer

Clouds

 Flying sauce

The Moon

can't remember

↓ Asteroid Belt

↑ Asteroid Belt Buckle

 The Moonie

Andromedary Spiral (a camel galaxy with two humps)

Uranus

Another big bum in space

Rings of Saturn ↓

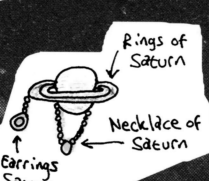

Pluto (used to be a planet, but in 2006 it was downgraded to the status of Cartoon Dog)

Necklace of Saturn

↑ Earrings of Saturn

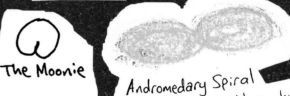 UFO

 No, UFO!

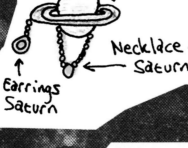 nepTunes This planet stores up to 14 light years worth of digital music

 Mercury (ask your dad)

o Mrs Pettigrew from number 14 (her nephew named a star after her!)

 Total eclipse of the heart (ask your Mum)

 Vulcan

 Interstellar tape

the seven dwarf planets

Jupiter

The first probe to explore the dark side of Patrick Moore's head.

Blupeter (a planet they made earlier)

Planet of the Apes

Planet of the Spiders

Dog Star

Cat Star

this is a sausage

Space hopper

↑ Spilt Milky Way →

Hubble Telescope

Flying V-ness

A cloud of astronaut poo

Bubble Telescope

Venus

← Spiral Arm →

Black Hole (not much to look at, but very easy to draw)

Venus Fly-trap (spaceships look out!)

103

LITTLE HOWARD'S
Who's Who?

Little Howard's Autobiography

I am officially the only cartoon boy living in Purley. I live with Big Howard, a real man (sort of), and MOTHER, a computer who thinks she's our mother.

I was born eight years ago, on my sixth birthday (in cartoon boy years). I'm still six, and I've just celebrated my eighth sixth birthday. That's how it works with cartoon boys, apparently.

I am brilliant at everything, but there are *some* things I don't know about. When I don't know about something, like all the greatest minds in the world, I ask a Biiiiig Question about them and set off a Klaxon, which makes a big friend of mine jump and have an accident. It's the same with all great thinkers. Galileo Galilei (will you do the fandango?) did it, and nudged the bloke who was creating the Tower of Pisa, so now it leans. And I believe Stephen Hawking beeps the horn on his wheelchair when he has a brief question about the universe to ask, and sometimes, when he's round Stephen's house, this causes Carl Sagan to fall out the window (they are all brainy people by the way, who mainly talk about the universe and stuff).

I don't go to school because the local education authority decided that, if as the BBC decided that my home life was educational enough to be broadcast as part of their factual children's output, it was educational enough to qualify as home schooling. I don't have a nose or any ears. If you've got a problem with that you can go and put your face in a trifle.

Most likely to say:
'I, Little Howard, have come up with another of my Biiiiiig Questions!' (at least once a week, not including repeats)
'Sounds plausible…'
'Brilliaaant!'
'Oh monkey-doos!'
'You're a mean, mean pigeon.'
'I love monkeys!'

Least likely to say:
'To be honest, I'm not really interested.'
'We'd better not, we'll get in trouble.'
'Let's face it, we'll never know the answer to this one.'
'I can't find my klaxon!'

Keywords:
Funny
Questioning
Curious
Mischievous
Determined
Innocent
Grumpy
Sneaky
Noseless
Cartoon
Volatile

Big Howard's Biography
By Little Howard

Big Howard is my real, grown-up friend (who isn't that grown-up). Like most grown-ups he thinks he's clever and in charge, but he sometimes finds himself in an aeroplane doing a loop-the-loop, or pegged out to a hillside waiting to be abducted by aliens, when he was sure he said he definitely wasn't going to let that happen.

I think that even though Big Howard is very big, he's actually quite little inside. I sometimes think his body is actually a big robot suit and a tiny weeny little idiot boy lives inside him and moves his arms and legs about. That would explain why he's so clumsy.

Not a lot of people know that Big Howard was actually quite small when he was born. He got the name Big Howard though because his mother (the one who isn't a computer!) wasn't very good at telling whether things were big, or just very close to her face. His full name is Big Howard Oliver Drinkwater Read, but no one ever calls him that. Not without sniggering.

Big Howard was the biggest baby (or the closest to his mum's face) born in Hitchin in 1975. Despite being quite a lot smaller than he is now, he still had a head the shape of Frankenstein, as you can see.

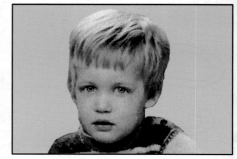

Big Howard then went to school, where he appeared to get smaller, but only because many boys at school were bigger

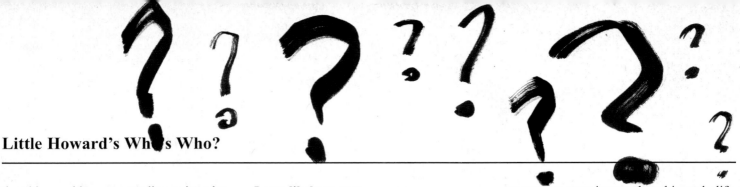

than him, and he was spending quite a lot of the day quite far away from his mum's face. Teachers were very impressed with Big Howard's school work, or at least the doodles he'd done in the margins next to his school work. They thought what he'd actually written was rubbish.

When Big Howard left school he had several qualifications under his belt, and several more stuffed up the front of his jumper. They were all teaching qualifications that he'd stolen from the wall of his headmaster's office, and I bet the frames were really uncomfortable on the bus home.

By this time Big Howard was very big. In fact too big for his mother. Whenever she saw him up close she ran away screaming that she was being attacked by a giant. So Big Howard had to leave home.

Somehow Big Howard managed to get into university. He did this by getting a daily visitor's pass and changing the date on it every day for three years. When he'd finished at university he had fewer degrees than a fridge-freezer, so he decided not to get a job but to be a standing-up comedian instead.

As a standing-up, Big Howard decided his main aim was to 'leave the audience wanting more'. He did this by spending as little time on stage as possible, so people wouldn't realize he wasn't very funny. Unfortunately this usually "left the audience wanting their money back." His motto was 'If you haven't got anything funny to say, don't say anything at all, and get off'.

Most likely to say:
'I do wish you wouldn't do that.'
'How many times have I told you not to attempt to build a nuclear reactor in the living room!?'
'Why do I ever ask you anything…?'
'Are you going to finish that treacle sponge?'
'What?!?!?!'

Least likely to say:
'Set off that klaxon again, please. Go on! I like it.'
'That's ok, it didn't hurt at all.'
'No more treacle sponge for me!'
'That's a very good question, Little Howard, let's answer it right now!'

Key words:
Big
Human
Accident-prone
Clumsy
Flappy
Gullible
Naïve
Simple
Dopey
Great big whiffy bumhead
(Yes thank you, Little Howard, that's enough key words about me.)

MOTHER's biography
By Little Howard

MOTHER hasn't always been a hyper-intelligent super-computer who can also get your washing done. In fact she has never been that, but she told me to say that in the first sentence or she'd triple-iron all my pants. She'll have stopped reading this now, so I can tell you that she is also a home computer who is convinced she's Big Howard's mother. This is very strange, but she is getting on a bit – MOTHER was actually born before home

computers were invented, and in early life she was an abacus, with several of its beads missing (because a girl had made them into a necklace).

She was then promoted to pocket calculator. Unfortunately, at the time, pocket calculators were only small enough to fit in the apron pocket of an elephant. Elephants however don't have very delicate feet (and most of them are brilliant at mental arithmetic), and CALCULATOR-MOTHER was soon crushed by her first owner Elmore (a young male African Elephant at Chester Zoo) who was trying to calculate how many apples he would have left if he ate four of his ten apples. But he ate them all anyway.

So MOTHER became a scientific calculator. Scientific calculators are specially advanced calculators for people who want to look clever. They have loads of extra buttons, and only evil scientists know what any of them do. It was as a scientific calculator that she said her first words, which was 'Boobies' when someone typed '5,318,008' on her, and then turned her upside down. Unfortunately someone pressed the Pi key and so her first message was misinterpreted as 'EblbBsEsg2bsi4i.E' and therefore ignored as just an upside-down number.

Some of MOTHER's un-smashed circuits ended up in one of the UK's first home computers. She could finally talk to people, if only by flashing up random messages like 'syntax error'. And people talked to her, though mainly just to say, 'Come on! Hurry up! You useless piece of junk!' She was very good however at destroying small rotating spaceships with quite unrealistic asteroids.

It was at this point that she met Big Howard, who bought her at a jumble sale because he needed a computer with a spell checker. Shortly after she moved into Big Howard's house he accidentally dropped a sherry trifle on MOTHER's motherboard, and it was at

this point she started talking and talking, and became convinced that she was his mother. And the rest is history! And like history, quite a lot of it is too boring to repeat.

Most likely to say:
'Oh dear, my DVD drive is full of Victoria Sponge mix. Yummy!'
'Hello Boys!'
'…And so you've completely wasted your time!'
'Botty Chocolate!' (first computer to say 'Botty chocolate' on the BBC, she's very proud of that)

Least likely to say:
'Now I don't want to cause any trouble...'
'Of course I'm not Big Howard's mother! I'm a computer, you idiot!'
'I'm not completely sure that I'm correct about this...'

Key words:
Maternal
Mental
Erratic
Inappropriate
Gossipy
Very clever
Very stupid

Roger's Biography
By Roger T. Pigeon (but I wrote it like someone else wrote it, because that makes you sound more important – NB: DON'T PRINT THAT BIT – say it

was written by Melvyn Bragg, or someone off *Newsround* or something; all clever and impressive, like.)

Roger T. Pigeon is Big Howard and Little Howard's sole agent. They are forbidden to find work through anyone else, and there are very stiff penalties if this rule is not observed. By which I mean they are forced to do penalty shoot-outs in suits of armour.

Roger was hatched, from a bad egg, in a nest wedged in the extractor fan of the Gents' toilet on the southbound platform of Barnsley station, just before the Great Fumigation of 1974. From an early age he was an enterprising young business-pigeon. At the age of just three months he made his first shiny sixpence by shaving his younger sister Gladys while she slept, and selling her feathers to a man who wanted to make a tiny pillow (so he could get to sleep on the night train to King's Cross). It's often said that Roger would sell his own granny for a quick wad of cash – well, the truth is he sold her years ago (she was ridiculously old and he had no further use for her, it was sound economic common sense), and has been counterfeiting grannies ever since for the lucrative granny market in the Far East (Hull).

Roger flew the nest at a young age, or rather was vibrated out of it by the southbound 8.38 to Birmingham New Street. However, the narrow-waisted, good-looking young pigeon landed on his feet – on the roof of buffet car, where he lived in a cupboard under the sandwich toaster in a nest made out of sugar sachets and coffee stirrers, until he learned to fly. They say that travel broadens the mind, but if you live on a train in a cupboard under a sandwich toaster, it also broadens the body.

Roger was made nestless when the spotty fool who ran the buffet car ran out of cups one day, and looked in the cupboard under the sandwich toaster for the first time.

Roger found himself all alone on the streets of King's Cross station. For three years Roger literally scratched out a living pecking at rubbish on the main concourse outside Whistlestop Food and Wine. It was here that he developed his familiar gravelly voice. By the age of five he was already eating at least five packets of cigarettes a day! (NOTE FROM BIG HOWARD: SMOKING CIGARETTES CAN VERY SERIOUSLY DAMAGE YOUR HEALTH. EATING THEM IS JUST STUPID).

Forced out of his home in the station's clock tower when the minute hand pushed his nest off its perch on the hour every hour for three months, he finally decided to up sticks (lolly sticks, dog hair and bits of crisp wrapper) and move on. He took up residence in the fold in the top of Admiral Nelson's hat, at the top of the column in Trafalgar Square. It is here that he founded Roger T. Pigeon Enterprises. The company was initially set up as a protection firm, requesting tourists to pay a fee or they would be pooed on while posing for photos. But times grew hard and Roger had to move downmarket into theatrical management.

As an agent and manager for actors, actresses, singers and 'actresses', Roger met, and soiled the windscreens of, nearly everyone in showbiz. He had nests near the stage doors of all the London theatres, and attended all the big premieres and openings, rubbing shoulders (and spreading lice) among the glitterati and dive-bombing the hats of royalty.

Roger became Big Howard and Little Howard's agent in 2001 when he saw them at the Edinburgh fringe festival, and has been sacked and re-appointed nearly two hundred times since then but ultimately they know that they need him a LOT more than he needs them.

If anybody asks you did NOT see Roger in this book, ok.

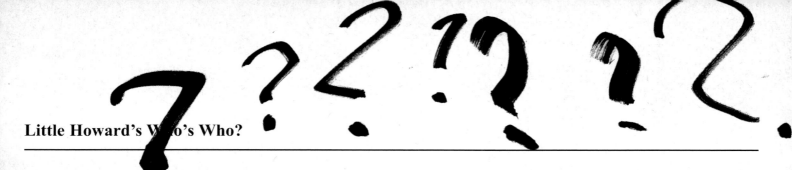

Little Howard's Who's Who?

Most likely to say:
'Oh feathers!'
'Look at the plumage on that!'
'Oi! Flappy Legs! Kiss my tail feathers!'

Least likely to say:
'No, I insist. I'll pay for this one!'
'…Now, I don't want to be unreasonable…'
'Isn't that a little… dishonest?'

Key words:
Pigeon
Mean mean Machiavellian
Greedy
Baddie
Show stealer

Little Susan's Biography
By Little Howard

Until now very little was known about Little Susan. She was a riddle, wrapped in a mystery, inside an enigma from Croydon. But in a recent interview she opened up about her past for the first time. She is definitely NOT just me in a wig.

Little Susan was drawn in Croydon and found herself living with a grown-up human lady, also called Susan. It was a long time though before they became known as 'Little Susan and Tall Susan'. For a long time they were just called Susan and Susan, or 'the two Susans', and whenever anyone got confused which Susan someone was talking about people would just say, 'You know, the cartoon one,' or, 'You know, the one that isn't a cartoon'. Some people called them 'Human and Cartoon Susan' but that didn't really have much of a ring to it. It was only when they met me and Big Howard that they became known as 'Big Susan and Little Susan'. They were called this because Roger T. Pigeon encouraged them to steal our stage act. The name was quickly changed for copyright reasons, and because Tall Susan, for some reason, didn't like being called 'Big'.

Some people say that I'm in love with Little Susan, but I'm definitely not, obviously, so shut up. We met when Big Howard started going out with Tall Susan, and as the only cartoon boy and girl in Purley we got on very well. Our relationship went a bit wonky when Big Howard and Tall Susan split up over allegations that Tall Susan and Little Susan were performing all of our jokes on stage, in higher voices, and getting more laughs and money. But in series 2 and 3 we patch up our differences and together continue to enjoy such activities as dressing up as monkeys, throwing vegetables at Big Howard and competing in the international world championship finals of Swingballdon.

Little Susan enjoys throwing things at Big Howard (who doesn't?), particularly cabbages and tomatoes, and removing her hair and doing an impression of an egg. She is a sweet and clever, and has got nice eyes, but she gets a bit grumpy if she think anyone's doing anything too naughty. It says here she is interested in steam trains and sumo wrestling, but that can't be right surely.

Most likely to say:
Very little.
'Yay! Let's play lob-veg!'
'But that's a stupid idea.'
'I am a egg!'
'Noorrrrr'
'Can't you all just grow up a bit?'

Least likely to say:
Very much.
'I don't think we should throw a pumpkin at him, won't that hurt?'
'That egg impression's getting a bit tired now Little Howard.'
'Oi, you old cow, gimme your pension book or I'll cut you up.'

Keywords:
Funny
Sweet
Feisty
Nice
Lob-veg

Advertisement

RtP Productions presents...
THE PORTABLE PICNIK ENHANCEMENT SAFETY + tRAVEL PACK™

INC
* SOUP STABILIZER
* BUTTER BELT
* EGG STRAPS
* GRAVY GOGGLES
* GAMMON HARNESS
... EVERYTHING YOU NEED FOR A SAFE PICNIC!

* PIGEON-PROOF PARASOL SOLD SEPERATELY

twittyface
friendtube

Big Howard's Rolling Status Feed

BigHoward

Big Howard and Little Howard are now friends.
6 hours ago via web

 Little Howard had a nice day at the seaside, but reckons a jumbo sherbert ice lolly wasn't too much to ask.
5 hours ago via RaspBerry®

 Little Susan I agree!
5 hours ago via web

 Big Howard Look, as I explained in person, there was a casserole in the oven.
5 hours ago via iGnome

 Little Howard But an ice lolly isn't food, it's a frozen drink. Besides, the casserole was horrible.
5 hours ago via RaspBerry®

 Big Howard I'm not discussing this on a social networking site.
5 hours ago via iGnome

Big Howard and Little Howard are now not friends anymore.
5 hours ago via iGnome

Big Howard and Little Howard are now friends again.
4 hours ago via iGnome

 MOTHER doesn't know what went wrong with the casserole!!! ;)
4 hours ago via web

 Mrs Pettigrew from Number 14 Ooh dear, not another one ruined!!
4 hours ago via MonkeyBadger®

 MOTHER Tell me about it!!! CGA
4 hours ago via web

 Mrs Pettigrew from Number 14 What's CGA, dear?
4 hours ago via MonkeyBadger®

 MOTHER Currently Giggling Audibly. Duhhh!!
4 hours ago via web

 Mrs Pettigrew from Number 14 Well there's no need for that, I don't understand all this RLOLTF IMHVP nonsense.
3 hours ago via MonkeyBadger®

Big Howard Easy now. MOTHER, I think the problem was you didn't use a Pyrex dish.
3 hours ago via iGnome

 MOTHER Oops!!
2 hours ago via web

 Big Howard You used my slippers.
2 hours ago via iGnome

 MOTHER Tsk!!
2 hours ago via web

 Mrs Pettigrew from Number 14 Sorry luv, bit touchy earlier. Mr Pettigrew got back from snooker early.
2 hours ago via MonkeyBadger®

 MOTHER Say no more, dear.
2 hours ago via web

 Big Howard You actually used my slippers.
2 hours ago via iGnome

 Roger T. Pigeon Variety Artistes is attending the event Roger T. Pigeon Presents... 'A Night of Keiths'
'For the first time ever, an evening of spectacular entertainment delivered entirely by men called Keith. 2 singers, a magician, a juggler, a comic, and an entire urban contemporary dance troupe. All called Keith.'
1 hour ago via web

 Little Susan LOL what?! That sounds rubbish!
52 minutes ago via web

 Little Howard Yeah, Roger – that is a rubbish idea.
32 minutes ago via RaspBerry®

 Roger T. Pigeon Variety Artistes You dozy kids wouldn't know entertainment if it came up to you in the street and said, 'Hello, my name's Keith.'
28 minutes ago via web

 Big Howard No, they're right, Roger, it is a really, really rubbish idea.
22 minutes ago via iGnome

 MOTHER The magician called Keith is very good. I still can't work out where he hid my purse.
18 mintes ago via web

 Roger T. Pigeon Variety Artistes > Big Howard All right, smarty pants. The comic called Keith has got measles. I'll give you £20 each if you go on as Big Keith and Little Keith.
10 minutes ago via web

 Big Howard > Roger T. Pigeon Variety Artistes You're on.
5 minutes ago via iGnome

 Boy Down The Swings is down the swings.
2 minutes ago via DaveBerry®

LITTLE HOWARD'S SUPER HEROES

SUUUU-PER HEEEE-ROES! EVERYONE LOVES THEM. I TOLD BIG HOWARD I WOULD DO A BRILLIANT SUPER HERO COMIC STRIP HERE, BUT IT TURNS OUT I CAN'T DRAW PEOPLE MOVING. SO I MIGHT HAVE TO GET BIG HOWARD TO DRAW A COMIC STRIP FOR ME. IN THE MEANTIME, ENJOY THESE SUPER HEROES STANDING STILL!

BOGEYMAN

TM & © 1987 ROGER T. PIGEON

* Ejects super-sticky green muco-slime over the enemy.
* That's it.
* Arch Rivals:
  Captain Snotty
  The Nasal Avenger
  Tissue Boy
  Kleenexicon

* Breaks up scuffles in dinner queue with a single bound.
* Iron giant mash scoop.
* Super Vision!!!
* Imperishable rubber gloves

magic weapons

armour-plated tabard

DINNER LADY

TM & © 1987 ROGER T. PIGEON

OLDMAN

TM & © 1987 ROGER T. PIGEON

* Melvin Parbold is a fit, healthy 12-year-old boy. But when he eats a Werthers Original, he turns into Oldman, a 73-year-old crimefighter. He can't run, he can't walk very fast, jumping is a no-no. Actually, he's not much of a superhero to be honest.

BEETLEBUM

TM & © 1987 ROGER T. PIGEON

* Beetlebum was in an accident in space and ended up with a stag beetle's abdomen sticking out where his backside should be!

* He lays his eggs in dead tree stumps.

* Can climb about halfway up a wall.

111

MOTHER's
>>Hectic Social Calendar!<<

MONDNESDAY 32TH SEPTOBER

9am: Hairdressers. Circuits permed.

11am: Organize 'Mums V Toddlers All-In Wrestling' at the drop-in centre

12.30pm: Local Council Meeting

IDEAS:
- Broader broadbands for the larger Internet user
- Anything to do with jam
- Edible clothes for the homeless?
- Put curtains round statues so they can get some sleep
- Get Cadbury to launch a long swirly caramel chocolate bar just for the Purley Ladies
  Rugby Team: the Swirly Purley Burly Girlie Curly Wurly.

6.30pm: Bluetooth Jiu-Jitsu 2.0

11pm: Shutdown.

TUEDNESDAY 33ST SEPTOBER

9am: Beautician. Mousemat waxed.

11am: Judge Purley's Nicest Concrete Toadstools competition.

11.30am: Make a stew out of Purley's Nicest Concrete Toadstools.

2pm: Gym. Squash with Mrs P, crunches with Mrs E, and splatter with Mr X.

7pm: To the theatre! Him From That Thing stars in a new musical about That Band From the Seventies. Can't wait!!

WENSDAY 34ND SEPTOBER

9am: Tanning Salon. Keyboard bronzed.

10.30am: Tea, Scones, Tea, Tea, Scones, Scones, Tea and Coffee Morning for Young Mums at the drop-out Centre. Bring moussaka.

11.30am: Shops. Return faulty toaster (nothing in the manual about not keeping small change in it).

4pm: Remember to remind self to remember that thing I said I'd remember.

6pm: Do the ironing.

6.10pm: Do the dishes.

6.20pm: Iron the dishes.

6.30pm: Dish the irons?

THURNEDSDAY 35TD SEPTOBER

9am: Nail bar. Bar nailed to door.

11am: Organize Extreme Sports for Newborn Babies at the drop-off centre.

1pm: Make up rumours about neighbours and spread them, eg:
- The bull terrier at Number 36 is having an affair with Number 47's shitsu.
- Mr and Mrs Windsor's youngest is no better than he should be.
- The satellite dish at Number 11 receives messages from space, because the Robinsons are in fact alien beings planning to take over the world.

2pm: Hide from neighbours.

5pm: Attempt a risotto.

6pm: Attempt another risotto.

7pm: Abandon risotto. Corned beef sandwiches instead. Yum!

9pm: That lovely film I like is on telly. Must set the video to set the DVD recorder to set the Sky Plus box to remind me to watch it.

FRINEDSDAY 317EENTH SEPTOBER

REBOOTS AND PANTIES

ROGER T. PIGEON presents his...

VARIETY ARTISTES

PATTY MONGREW
(The singer with the sniffles)

'Patty's a real gem, in that I found her in a hole underground. She's been making a name for herself (out of plywood) for donkey's years, one look at her tells you that, but now her star is really set to rise and shine, like the sun, which after all is a star – a great big fat yellow one. Just like Patty.

'Patty sings like a semi-professional angel, but her smashing unique selling point is that she's always got the sniffles. This gives her voice a very dramatic emotional effect. I have to leave the room when she sings *Bright Eyes*. Mainly because I hate it.'

THE NUISANCE TWINS

'Griff and Vance Nuisance are break-dancing twins with a difference – they were born several years apart to different parents. They learnt their fancy moves on the mean streets of Dorking, but they didn't stop at break-dancing! Snap-jigging, crunch-twirling, shatter-pirouetting, there's no end to the number of hyphenated synonyms these lads have mastered.

'Griff overcame a wig injury and gave up a promising career as a sewage attendant to pursue his dream of dancing in a funny way for not much money. Vance, on the other hand, was born break-dancing. Which may have been why the midwife dropped him on his head. Unless he started break-dancing because she dropped him on his head, I'm not really sure.'

THE RAVISHING UMBUNGO AND ADRIAN

'A real class act, these two. The Ravishing Umbungo comes from the mystic splendour of the Near East (Orpington), and studied Silly Tricks under the great Oomi Gewleys. Adrian is a remarkable young ex-librarian from the Amazon who rollerblades like a gazelle. On rollerblades. After it's learned how to rollerblade.

'Together they have entertained all the crowned heads of Europe, including a booking to headline the French Royal Variety Performance. Sadly, the event was cancelled when the French remembered they'd cut all their royal family's heads off 200 years ago.'

FLORACITY

'I'm very excited to have snagged these fellas, the most exciting and radical team of urban flower arrangers that the world never knew it didn't need. All seven of them are from tower blocks, which means they're raw and street and hip and I can pay them next to nothing.

"They went to Covent Garden with their mum aged ten and noticed a space between two stalls. Immediately they'd spotted a gap in the market. They first came to my attention when they planted a sequence of rhododendrons and clematis in a wickerwork pot to symbolize the problem of gang violence in our inner cities."

LUKE HARRIS'S UNNECESSARILY VAST GUITAR

'I couldn't believe my eyes when I discovered this little lad in a pub car park playing a colossally oversized electric guitar with the aid of a stepladder and a broomstick.

'He's a very good player on normal-sized guitars, but he can't even strum the most basic tune on this giant instrument. Never mind, just watching him continually fall off the stepladder is entertainment enough. He got his head caught between strings once. I wept. It was *hilarious*.'

SARCASTICAT

'Think she's a cute fluffy moggy? Think again! That's Sarcasticat, the Most Sarcastic Cat in the World! Obviously I've never actually met Sarcasticat – she's a cat! They don't like me, and the feeling's mutual. But I've watched her on stage and even from a distance the amount of sarcasm she packs into a miaow has to be heard to be believed.

'For an encore she invites the audience to stroke her and does an 'ironic purr' which makes everyone feel strangely belittled. I'm currently starting a petition for Sarcasticat to replace Vernon Kay on *Family Fortunes*. That would be brilliant.'

Little Howard's Song Lyrics

WHY DOES TIME FLY WHEN YOU'RE HAVING FUN?

LITTLE HOWARD
When it's dull it lasts forever,
When it's fun it goes too quick,
I sometimes think that Father Time
Is trying to take the mick.

BIG HOWARD
If we could make good things last longer,
Blimey that would be a trick.

BOTH
Why does time fly when you're having fun?

DORIS
When you're young life goes too slowly,
When you're old it goes too fast.
Happy moments only seem to roll into the past.
But I have found a way that
We can make the good times last,
Try doing something new and scary every day!

LITTLE HOWARD
I could punch an anaconda!

DORIS
Or just learn the clarinet.

LITTLE HOWARD
I could wrestle a gorilla

DORIS
Or do something for a bet.

LITTLE HOWARD
I could goose a big chinchilla.

BIG HOWARD:
Or even better yet,
Try doing something safe but scary every day!

LITTLE HOWARD
When it's dull life goes too slowly,
When it's fun it goes too fast,
Happy moments only seem to rush into the past
If only we could find a way that
We could make the good times last,

DORIS
Try doing something safe but scary every day!

LITTLE HOWARD
I could change my name to 'Farty'.

BIG HOWARD
Now that I'd like to see.

LITTLE HOWARD
I could join the Labour Party

BIG HOWARD
Liberal, Green and then Tory.

LITTLE HOWARD
I could learn black belt karate

BIG HOWARD
But don't go kicking me.

BOTH
Let's try something safe but scary every day.

INSTRUMENTAL

ALL
But I have found a way that we can
make the good times last,
Try doing something new and scary every day!

LITTLE HOWARD
I could ask out Mrs Jackson!

BIG HOWARD
That's a teacher at your school!

LITTLE HOWARD
I could buy a louder klaxon!

BIG HOWARD
Who invited this old fool?

LITTLE HOWARD
I could wrestle Jeremy Paxman!

BIG HOWARD
Now that really would be cool!

LITTLE HOWARD
Try doing something safe but scary –

BIG HOWARD
(spoken)
Something safe but scary

BOTH
Doing something safe but scary every day.

AT LEAST YOU'RE NOT ME!

UNLUCKY LES:
They say that good things always come to those who wait,
But if that's true,
Mine's running late.
Had so much bad luck it's a crime,
But at least it's here on time,
At least you're not me,
At least you're not me,
At least you're not me.

CHORUS
At least you're not me,
At least you're not me.
At least you are you,
So don't be blue, you could be me.

UNLUCKY LES:
They say that lightning never strikes the same place twice,
If that was true,
That would be nice.
But I've found that lightning strikes,
Wherever lightning likes,
It usually strikes me,
It usually strikes me,
At least you're not me.

At least you're not me,
At least you're not me.
At least you are you,
So don't be blue, you could be me.

They say that bad things always come to you in threes,
If that was true,
I would be pleased,
It seems with me bad things are able,
To come in all the three-times table,
At least you're not me,
At least you're not me,
At least you're not me.

At least you're not me, (LH: I'm glad I'm not you)
At least you're not me. (LH: I'm glad I'm not you)
At least you are you,
So don't be blue, you could be me.

LITTLE HOWARD:
Your words will really help to get me through,
I'm very glad, that I'm not you!
But Les what do you do?
As I'm pretty sure you're you,
I'm sure that you're you,
I'm sure that you're you,
I'm sure that you're you.

LES [SPOKEN]
Good point well made, Little Howard.
I am me.And always have been.
I like to think of luck like this.
What's your favourite drink, Little Howard?

LITTLE HOWARD [SPOKEN]:
I like orange juice.

LES [SPOKEN]:
Good choice. I prefer something a bit
stronger myself.

LITTLE HOWARD [SPOKEN]:
What?! Orange juice with bits in?

LES [SPOKEN]:
Yes, if you like, orange juice with bits in.

LITTLE HOWARD [SPOKEN]:
Wow! Now there's a man who can handle
His vitamin C!

UNLUCKY LES [SUNG]:
Luck is like a glass of orange juice,
With the finest bits,
Man can produce.
And I know some have got a fuller glass than me,
But would prefer,
A cup of tea.
I don't have much luck to waste,
But at least I like the taste,
I'm glad that I'm me,
I'm glad that I'm me,
I'm glad that I'm me.

LES & LITTLE HOWARD:
I'm glad that I'm me,
I'm glad that I'm me,

I'm glad that I'm me,
I'm glad that I'm me,
I'm glad that I'm me,

I'm glad that I'm me,
I'm glad that I'm me,
I'm glad that I'm me.

121

REJECTED BIG QUESTIONS:

How hard can it be, performing brain surgery?

Can I eat an aeroplane?

 How do they turn cows into beef burgers?

Which is the one true God?

Can I go abroad at some point? Please?

Who killed Big Howard?

What's for tea?

Why are Scottish people so angry?

What were Genghis Khan's good points?

Which is the best street gang?

Can I join N-Dubz?

 Can I become a girl?

How many grains of sand are there on the beach at Margate?

What happens in a nuclear war?

What are the possible ramifications of changing my name to 'Peter Shilton'?

Which motorway is best? And are we nearly there yet?

As we're running out of ideas, could the dinosaurs ever come back again?

Can I form a people's army and seize control of the state?

What happens if I press this button?

DON'T PRESS!!

Which of these two milkshakes contains deadly cyanide?

If the sum of the hypotenuse is equal to the sum of the square on the other two sides, why is a mouse when it spins?

> Quite a lot of my ideas for *Big Questions* weren't allowed to be shown on TV, which is very annoying, as most of them are better than the ones we did. So sit back and imagine how *Big* Howard and I might have dealt with these humdingers!

Little Howard
and the
Magic Pencil of LIFE and Death
Big Howard and Little Howard's unique live show, coming to a theatre near you soon!
Little Howard discovers the pencil that created him, and the rubber on the other end that could DESTROY him!
With brand new characters, jokes and with more twists than a game of Twister with an octopus, this show takes Little Howard to a whole new dimension (hint hint)!
"I defy you not to be helplessly charmed"
The Telegraph
'incredibly, achingly funny'
The Daily Mail
'This has to be one of the most magical double acts on the circuit,'
The Stage
'the best show we've seen at the Edinburgh Fringe Festival'
Families Magazine
'It appeals to both kids and adults... like The Simpsons'
Chortle.co.uk
For future tour dates and booking information go to www.littlehoward.co.uk

Contents.

125

Another Note From the (ex) Publisher

Dear Reader,

Hello, I'm Scott the ex-Publisher and I'd just like to say this is the last book I am ever going to publish. Editing this book and trying to get pages off of Big Howard and Little Howard has been difficult enough – we've never SEEN so many spelling mistakes (I was up until FOUR O'CLOCK EVERY MORNING FOR MONTHS correcting all of them – I hope) and they once sent us a load of wrapping paper and insisted that pages 42-97 could be decorated with a repeating pattern of reindeers throwing snowballs.

BUT trying to negotiate with their horrible, money-grabbing, so-called manager, Roger T. Pigeon, has been a COMPLETELY MAJOR SCREAMING NIGHTMARE. As have all the many long hours the whole office has put in trying to make MOTHER's printer work.

Put simply, this book has NEARLY COMPLETELY RUINED MY LIFE. When my bosses saw the material we were getting from the authors – especially the eighteen-page pull-out pictorial spread called 'Little Howard Sketches the Guffs of Insects', which is NOT in the final draft – they threatened to throw me out of the building after pouring the fish tank down my trousers. Yet I stood up for these USELESS IDIOTS.

But NO MORE. In a way I'd like to thank Little Howard and Big Howard, if not the other two, who I despise unreservedly. Because if this stupid book hadn't come into my life, I might never have realized that what I really wanted to do was to cut myself off from society forever, and live in a cave on the Yorkshire Moors.

Bye then,
Scott

Scott Pack
Ex-Publisher
The Friday Project

And I don't look
ANYTHING like that.

The F͟_____s Publishers . 77-85 Fulham Palace Road . ___don . W6 8JB

ridayproject.co.uk